"I'm Lisa's father and I want to be part of her life.

"For always," Gavin said. "Now that I know about her, she's my responsibility as much as yours."

"What does that mean?" Jessie asked. "You can't just suddenly upset her whole world! She's happy and well adjusted and I want her to stay that way."

The pain of Jessie's words went deeper than any pain he'd ever known. "I want to get to know Lisa. I won't tell her I'm her father until we both decide the time is right. I won't hurt her," Gavin vowed.

Jessie stood then. "I need a few days to think about this. All right?" At the corridor, she paused. "I will call you, Gavin. I truly want what's best for our daughter."

Gavin's heart lightened just a little. She'd used the words *our daughter.* That was a beginning.

Dear Reader,

From classic love stories to romantic comedies to emotional heart tuggers, Silhouette Romance offers six irresistible novels every month by some of your favorite authors—and some sure to become favorites. Just look at the lineup this month:

In *Most Eligible Dad,* book 2 of Karen Rose Smith's wonderful miniseries THE BEST MEN, a confirmed bachelor becomes a FABULOUS FATHER when he discovers he's a daddy.

A single mother and her precious BUNDLE OF JOY teach an unsmiling man how to love again in *The Man Who Would Be Daddy* by bestselling author Marie Ferrarella.

I Do? I Don't? is the very question a bride-to-be asks herself when a sexy rebel from her past arrives just in time to stop her wedding in Christine Scott's delightful novel.

Marriage? A very happily *un*married police officer finally says "I do" in Gayle Kaye's touching tale *Bachelor Cop.*

In *Family of Three* by Julianna Morris, a man and a woman have to share the same house—with separate bedrooms, of course....

Debut author Leanna Wilson knows no woman can resist a *Strong, Silent Cowboy*—and you won't be able to, either!

I'd love to know what you think of the Romance line. Are there any special kinds of stories you'd like to see more of, less of? Your thoughts are very important to me—after all, these books are for you!

Sincerely,

Melissa Senate,
Senior Editor

Please address questions and book requests to:
Silhouette Reader Service
U.S.: 3010 Walden Ave., P.O. Box 1325, Buffalo, NY 14269
Canadian: P.O. Box 609, Fort Erie, Ont. L2A 5X3

MOST ELIGIBLE DAD

Karen Rose Smith

Silhouette
ROMANCE™
Published by Silhouette Books
America's Publisher of Contemporary Romance

To Edie—thank you for your friendship and
continuing support.

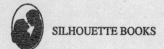 SILHOUETTE BOOKS

ISBN 0-373-19174-X

MOST ELIGIBLE DAD

Copyright © 1996 by Karen Rose Smith

KAREN ROSE SMITH

created scenes in her mind when she was a teenager to fit popular songs. Those scenes developed into stories. Reading romances has been a favorite pastime throughout her life. Her love for the genre led her to apply the skills of her English degree to writing romances after back surgery. Now, she cannot imagine doing anything else. She says, "I try to write stories about hope and overcoming obstacles. My characters are as real to me as my friends. I share their pain as well as their joy and cheer them on as they resolve their conflicts."

Karen hopes you enjoy meeting Cade, Gavin and Nathan—the three special men from her "Best Men" series. She likes hearing from her readers. You can write to her at P.O. Box 1545, Hanover, PA 17331.

Gavin Bradley's Tips on Becoming a Surprise Dad

1. When you discover you're a father, do not blow up at the mother of your child—this is not proper daddy behavior.

2. Though you want to claim your child, have patience. She's got to get to know you—and like you—before she can love you.

3. Try your darnedest to win over your child's mother. After all, she is the woman you've never forgotten.

4. When it's time to propose, ask them both to help you create a new family. And do whatever you must so they'll both say yes!

Prologue

Gavin Bradley's mind was not on the newly acquired diploma he placed in the suitcase on his bed. His thoughts were on Jessie Windsor and how he couldn't wait to see her again.

Last night had been the most wonderful night of his life. He should be sorry their kisses and touches had gotten out of hand. He should have been prepared. But after he'd dated her for four months, keeping a tight rein on his control, constantly telling himself this was the wrong time to fall in love because of med school looming ahead, their desire had suddenly exploded.

Maybe it was because they'd known their graduation today represented a milestone in their lives. Maybe it was because Jessie was going home with her father this afternoon, and it would be at least a few weeks until they could see each other again. Maybe it was because he'd never fallen in love like this before. He thought about her during the day. At night he dreamed about stroking her long, light brown hair, feeling the caring and passion in her beautiful blue eyes and her kisses....

An unexpected knock sounded at Gavin's door. His fraternity brothers were either out celebrating with their families or on their way home. Gavin didn't have those options. Just as he couldn't take a few days off. He had a job that started Monday and was leaving for Pennsylvania early tomorrow morning. He'd be working in a factory on the outskirts of the town where he'd start med school in September. He'd be putting in long hours, making as much money as he could for school, but maybe Jessie could drive up some weekend. Maybe he could visit her over Labor Day.

He strode to the door, thinking his visitor might be Jessie, come to say another goodbye. After the graduation ceremony, he'd only managed a hug before she'd run off to look for her father.

But when Gavin opened his door, he found a man in his fifties, dressed in a navy pin-striped suit, holding a manila folder. The man's wire-rimmed glasses sat high on his nose. His gray hair swept across his forehead as if he'd just stepped from the barber's chair. Everything about him was . . . precise.

"I'm looking for Gavin Bradley," the older man said, his expression serious.

"That's me. How can I help you?"

"I'm Owen Windsor, Jessica's father."

Gavin saw the resemblance then, in the straightness of Owen Windsor's nose and in the blue of his eyes. But that was as far as it went. Jessie was refined—Gavin had realized that from the moment he'd literally bumped into her at the Student Union Building. But she was also gentle, compassionate, with a touch of vulnerable innocence that made her special. There was nothing gentle, compassionate, vulnerable or innocent about her father.

Gavin motioned the man inside. "It's a pleasure to meet you. It was hard to find anyone in that crowd today. I thought you and Jessie would be on your way home."

Owen stepped into the room, pulled out the desk chair and sat on it, as if this were his room rather than Gavin's. "Jessica is still packing. She doesn't know I'm here."

Gavin sat on the bed across from Jessie's father. This wasn't an I'm-glad-you're-dating-my-daughter visit. "Why *are* you here?"

Without a preliminary explanation, Owen opened the folder in his hand and stared at Gavin with ice blue eyes that didn't resemble Jessie's at all. "I want you to understand who I am, who Jessica and I *are*. I graduated from Princeton. By age thirty I owned one plastics company. Now I own five. I'm on the board of Four Oaks Community Hospital and several charity organizations. I have considerable influence in the State of Virginia." He looked down at the open file. "Then there is you."

Gavin had fought all his life to head toward a future different from his past. He was proud of what he'd accomplished, and he held his head high in front of Owen Windsor now. "I'm a college graduate and I'm going to become a doctor. Has Jessie told you that?"

"It doesn't matter what Jessica has told me. What I know is that *you* grew up in the poorest section of Richmond. I know that your father was an alcoholic, and your mother was illiterate until the day she died. You have no living relatives, let alone two dimes to rub together. I doubt if you'll succeed in medical school. Scholarships have paid your way until now. You'll have to support yourself, as well as study, then pay back loans for years to come. Just what do you think you have to offer my daughter?"

Gavin had never been in love before, had never felt about anyone the way he felt about Jessie. But he knew better than Owen Windsor that love couldn't pay the bills or make up for lost dreams. Jessie's father sat before him, asking Gavin the question he should have asked himself. Jessie hadn't told Gavin much about her background. He knew her mother and father were divorced and she lived with her father. From her language, her clothes and her bearing, he'd realized her upbringing had been very different from his. They hadn't talked about the past because they'd been too absorbed in the present, enjoying every moment they could steal together.

Maybe he'd been afraid to ask the question Owen Windsor had posed to him. Maybe he'd been afraid to see what Jessie's father was explicitly pointing out. Depending on scholarships, studying, taking out loans, working his tail off with supplemental jobs to survive, Gavin knew the next eight years would be even worse than the past four. The conclusion was obvious. He had *nothing* to offer a woman like Jessica Windsor.

Owen looked Gavin straight in the eye. "The best thing you can do for my daughter is to leave her alone. If you don't, I'll make sure you never get your medical degree. Jessica is going to marry a man of breeding with more to offer her than years of hardship and loan installments."

Although Gavin knew the man before him could probably make good his threat, he wouldn't let Windsor intimidate him. But loving Jessie as he did, thinking of the years to come, wanting only the best for her, he realized there was only one thing he could do—stop seeing her, stop falling deeper in love than he already was.

With an arch of his eyebrows, Owen closed the folder. "Have I made my position clear?"

Gavin stood, dismissing the man before Windsor tried to dismiss *him*. "I understand that we both want what's best for Jessie."

Owen got to his feet and walked to the door. "Keep away from her, Bradley. She's got a future that doesn't include the likes of you. I've protected Jessica all her life. And I'll do so until I die."

Watching the door close, Gavin thought again about everything Owen Windsor had said. There was no refuting the obvious. It would be years until he could support himself, let alone the woman he loved. He had to stop seeing Jessie. He had to put her out of his mind and out of his heart.

But he had to explain why. He couldn't let her go without her knowing the reason. Yet he realized if he saw her or even heard her voice, his resolve might crumble. He went to his desk, took out a piece of paper and began to write.

Chapter One

Nine years later

"Good night, honey."

"Good night, Mommy."

Jessie turned the light off in her daughter's bedroom and smiled. Lisa had only managed to postpone her bedtime fifteen minutes tonight.

As Jessie descended the steps to the first floor of her town house, the phone rang. She picked up the receiver in her living room.

"Jessica, I just came from the board meeting at the hospital."

Her father never identified himself. But then again, she could never mistake him for anyone else. "Did something unusual happen?"

His pause told her it had. "We were informed who would be taking over Winnichuk's practice while he decides whether or not he wants to retire."

Dr. Peter Winnichuk had been Jessie's pediatrician and he was now her daughter's. He and his wife had planned a three-month vacation that could possibly lead into his retirement. "Do we know him? Or is it a 'her'?"

"Gavin Bradley is coming to Four Oaks and taking over for Winnichuk on May 22."

Jessie almost dropped the phone. Although nine years had passed, in a flash she remembered every line and feature of Gavin's face, his slightly squared jaw, his lean cheeks, his intense gray eyes. So often she'd wondered what was behind the intensity. She remembered how she'd have to stand on her tiptoes to kiss him, the gentleness in his large hands, the strength of his arms, the sound of his deep voice.

"Jessica?"

She remembered that one night—their bodies joined.... Just as suddenly she relived the pain of waiting for a call that had never come.

"Jessica, what are you going to do?" her father demanded.

She took a deep breath and tried to sort her thoughts. "If he's practicing at the hospital, it will be difficult for me to avoid him. Dr. Winnichuk and I consult often. And with my office in the annex across the parking lot..."

"I mean, what are you going to do about Lisa?"

Over the years, Jessie hadn't felt any closer to her father than she had when she was a child, though she did understand him better. She'd accepted his help the year after Lisa was born so she could finish up her master's and still have plenty of time to mother her baby. But after that year, she'd established herself in her own practice and taken care of herself and her daughter without his help, suggestions or interference. When she'd put the down payment on this town house two years ago, she'd finally felt like her own woman.

"Dad, you just dropped a bomb in my lap. I have to think about this. I never thought I'd see Gavin again."

Her father responded, "I never thought you would, either. He knew you came from Four Oaks. He might be here because of you."

"I find that hard to believe," she murmured as an aching she'd thought had faded away squeezed her heart again. "He left me and he never looked back. Why would he come now? It must be a coincidence."

"And if it isn't?"

"Either way, I have to consider telling him about Lisa. But I won't do that until I'm sure he won't hurt her the same way he hurt me."

"You'll never be sure of that."

Jessie knew her father was thinking of her mother. She suspected he'd never remarried because the pain of her mother's abandonment had been too frightful to contemplate again. "Dad, as I've told you before, you'll have to trust my judgment."

"I don't want to see you or Lisa get hurt."

Her father had never been affectionate. As a young girl Jessie had thought that meant he didn't love her. But she'd learned love took many forms, and her father's manifested itself in his desire to protect her—whether it be with his money, his influence or his advice. "I know you don't. I'm not about to do anything rash. Let me handle it, Dad, all right?"

"The best thing for you would be to keep your distance."

"I'll think about it. Honestly, I will."

After she said goodbye to her father, Jessie realized her hands were shaking. She'd stayed composed with him, but she didn't have a clue as to how she was going to handle this situation. Most important she had to protect Lisa. Then she had to protect herself.

Take one day at a time, a comforting voice inside her insisted. *You decided to do that long ago. And you know it works.*

Yes, that philosophy had worked in the past. But now Gavin would be living in the same town as his daughter—the daughter he had no idea existed.

Gavin accepted the glass of punch one of the nurses handed him but kept his gaze on the double doors leading into the small reception room on the second floor of Four Oaks Community Hospital. Would Jessie come to Dr. Winnichuk's bon-voyage party? Would he recognize her? Would she remember the ending of his letter? "I love you, Jessie. I will always love you."

Nine years ago, he couldn't ask her to wait for him to make something of himself. That would have tied her to him as much as continuing to see her or writing to her. But he'd hoped she'd understand the implied message. He'd hoped it had eased the pain of breaking up. Most of all, he'd hoped she'd understand that he had to feel worthy of her love before calling her his own.

As Gavin shifted his gaze to the door again, above the guests who'd come to the gathering to wish Dr. Winnichuk a good cruise, his heart pounded. Memories he'd tucked away came forging back as Jessica Windsor stepped over the threshold and stopped to get her bearings. Her light brown hair was shorter now and waved along her cheeks. He remembered it flowing across her shoulders, the blond strands glowing in the sunlight.

Hot desire, old feelings, the remembrance of a dream, surged through him all at the same time.

Her gaze met his. He saw recognition, remembrance and then pain. She frowned and a neutral mask settled across her face. As she walked toward him, her mauve tailored suit subtly revealing as much as it concealed, he saw that she was even more poised than when he'd known her in college. But when she stood before him, her light floral scent teasing him, the warmth he'd remembered had disappeared from her eyes.

"Hello, Dr. Bradley. Welcome to Four Oaks." Her voice was cool, politely friendly, as if she were an official member of the welcoming committee instead of a woman he'd known intimately.

"Don't think I'm going to call you Miss Windsor, Jessie."

Soft pink colored her cheeks.

Before he'd decided to take over Dr. Winnichuk's practice, even temporarily, Gavin had first checked the phone book to make sure Jessie was living here, then found out through the grapevine that she'd never married.

He intended to find out everything he could about what was going on in her life now. The best way to do that was to start with her work. "I understand you're a speech therapist."

"Yes, I am. My office is in the annex."

Silence fell between them. It seemed rife with words never spoken, thoughts never expressed, and Gavin realized they couldn't begin again here, not in the midst of a crowd. "Jessie, could I talk with you privately? Maybe we could go to my office. . . ."

A beep sounded twice. It was his pager.

Jessie looked almost relieved.

"Dr. Winnichuk officially signed off this afternoon," Gavin explained. "I don't know how long this will take, but if you plan to stay for a while . . ."

She shook her head. "No. I have to get home. I just came by to say goodbye to Dr. Winnichuk."

He'd hoped to ease into an invitation to dinner. But circumstances urged him to seize the moment. "Have dinner with me tomorrow night."

Her cheeks turned an even lovelier pink. "I can't," she said.

That answer was too definite to let slip by. Had he been too hopeful that she could still have feelings for him? Could they salvage anything from the few months they'd shared so long ago? There was something he needed to know right now. "Are you involved with anyone?"

Her blue eyes grew wide at the question. "No. But I have . . . commitments."

Damn. He needed to talk with her but he had to get to the phone. "I have a referral Dr. Winnichuk suggested I give you. I wanted to talk to you about that, as well as . . . other things." Like the past. The future. But he didn't mention those now because instinct told him she'd run if he did. So he stuck to the professional. "I'll send the notes over to you tomorrow." Glancing at the double doors, he added, "I have to go. But we'll talk soon. All right?"

He saw reluctance in her eyes, but she nodded.

That was as good as he could get for now, he realized, leaving her standing there when he'd rather stay. As he crossed the room, he could feel her eyes on his back, and he wondered if she was remembering as vividly as he was another time, when there'd been no awkwardness between them, but rather desire and friendship and promise.

Jessie heaved a sigh of relief as Gavin strode off. He hadn't changed a bit except to become more mature, more handsome, more . . . overpowering. She'd come to this party with all her defenses firmly in place in case he appeared. The only problem was, once she'd gazed into Gavin's eyes, she'd felt twenty-one again.

Should she even entertain the idea of having dinner with him? Yet how else could she find out what kind of man he'd become? How else could she find out if it would be in Lisa's best interests to let him know he had a daughter?

If he asked her to dinner again, maybe she should accept. At least now she had time to think about it. At least now she could regroup and prepare.

Two days later, Jessie paced her office, a manila folder in her hand. There was no reason why she couldn't have a professional relationship with Gavin Bradley and keep him at a distance. *Right?* Right. And she wouldn't panic simply because he was going to meet with her in her office in fifteen minutes. Absolutely not.

Annoyed with herself, she sat at her desk and read the note that had come with the folder by messenger yesterday afternoon.

Jessie,
I understand you are the most highly recommended speech therapist in Four Oaks. I would appreciate it if you could look over this file and tell me if you think you can help this child. I'll meet you at your office at 8:30 tomorrow morning to consult with you. If the time doesn't suit, call me.

Gavin

She sighed.
Just hearing his voice two days ago had given her chills. And when she thought about how he had once touched her... *Get a grip, girl. If you're not careful, he'll find out about Lisa before you're ready.*

She needed more than a good grip. When she'd first seen him, nine years had slipped away and too many feelings had come rushing back. Physical sensations, murmurs in the dark, kisses behind the dorm . . . the way he'd left—without a word, without an explanation. She'd remembered the loss, the news of her pregnancy, the embarrassment of being an unwed mother in a tight-knit community like Four Oaks.

Focusing on the folder in front of her, she again reread the report inside. The school district's speech therapist had recommended private therapy over the summer for a six-year-old boy. Apparently twice-weekly sessions in the school setting had helped, but a summer without practice and professional feedback could set the child back.

Jessie examined the statistical data that told so little. Then she read the school therapist's notes. As she'd realized last night when she'd read the file for the first time, she knew she could help this child as she'd helped so many others. What she didn't know was how she'd feel when she'd have to consult with Gavin Bradley.

Gavin stood on the doorstep to Jessie's office and checked his watch—8:28 a.m. She might not have arrived yet. But when he tried the handle on the door, it opened. Stepping into a pleasant atmosphere, he appreciated her taste in decorating. Pale-blue-and-mauve flowered wallpaper graced two walls. The other two were painted the palest blue. Children's chairs and a table, as well as toys—blocks, puzzles and books—fit comfortably in one corner.

He went to the door that stood slightly ajar and rapped. Jessie appeared before him. She looked like a spring vision in a two-piece dress sprinkled with tiny colorful flowers.

"Come in, Gavin." Her voice was evenly polite again.

"No receptionist?" he asked, following her into the office, intrigued by the soft material of her flared skirt brushing against her legs. Very shapely legs.

"I prefer to make my own appointments. I check my machine in between sessions in case there's something I need to deal with immediately."

She picked up the folder on her desk and opened it. "I think I can help your patient. According to the therapist's notes, he's already making progress. With school out, he'll be more relaxed. That will help. Plus I can give him longer sessions. Do you want me to call his parents or do you want to do it?"

What he wanted was to wipe the coolness from her voice. "I'll call. The situation is touchy. Rodney's father doesn't see the need for additional sessions. The mother does."

"And Rodney's caught in the middle," Jessie added with a perceptiveness she'd always had.

"Exactly."

Jessie closed the folder and laid it on the desk again. "If his parents would like to come see me and talk with me beforehand, that's fine. Just give them my number. I need their cooperation. It would help Rodney if they're both involved."

"Only his mother has been helping him until now. The father thinks Rodney needs to grow up and the stuttering will wear off."

Jessie shook her head, and her eyes filled with compassion. "That rarely happens."

This was the Jessie that Gavin remembered—the one who was warm and soft and caring. "I'll tell Rodney's mother to convince her husband to talk to you. If anyone can make him understand, you can."

Jessie looked startled for a moment, then responded, "I'm not a miracle worker, Gavin."

He leaned closer to take in more of her perfume, to take in more of her. "Maybe not. But from what I hear, you're close to it. And more important I can see that you care."

Jessie gazed up at him, her blue eyes wide and...turmoiled.

Gavin couldn't help leaning closer and tipping her chin up with his thumb. He saw the flash of want in her eyes and he bent his head, needing to find out if there was something still there besides the distance that was so frustrating to break through. He knew the kiss could be a mistake, but it could also give him the answer he needed.

His lips met hers, and sparks burst into flame. Her soft moan gave him the freedom to wrap her in his arms and coax her lips apart with his tongue. She responded, stroking against him, and then—

Jessie pulled away abruptly. One look at her face told him he'd just taken three giant steps backward.

"You had no right to do that," she said, a slight tremor rocking her words.

"I don't think it's a matter of rights. I thought you wanted it as much as I did. I thought maybe you were as curious as I was."

"Curious?"

"To see if the fire is still there. And obviously it is."

She curled her fingers into her palms. "*Obviously* you don't know what you're talking about."

"Jessie . . ."

She stepped away from him. "I have no intention of picking up where we left off nine years ago."

"Jessie, I know breaking up was difficult. . . ."

"Difficult? I didn't even *know* we were breaking up. You didn't call, you didn't write. I had no way to get in touch with you. And you think I'm happy to see you again?"

The torrent of her words caught him by surprise. "I *did* write."

She stared into his gray eyes, searching for the truth. "I never received a letter."

"I mailed it the day after we graduated . . . before I left for Pennsylvania."

"And I'm supposed to believe you?" she asked with an incredulous lift of her brows.

He clasped her shoulders, needing her to believe him. "Did I ever lie to you?"

"I don't know, Gavin. I only knew you for four months."

Letting go of his grip, he raked his hand through his hair, considering telling her about her father's visit that day. But would she think he was lying about that, too? Would it even matter? "I wrote to you, Jessie."

"And what did you say?" she asked softly, with more curiosity now than anger.

"That I had nothing to offer you. That I couldn't ask you to scrimp through medical school and residency with me."

She frowned. "Let me get this straight. You wrote to me to break up with me?"

"I wrote to you to explain why the time wasn't right for us."

"In other words, you...you didn't want an...encumbrance while you were studying to be a doctor."

He saw the hurt in her eyes—a hurt so deep he might never be able to reach it. And he realized no matter what he said, she thought he'd broken up with her so he would have his freedom. How hollow it sounded now to say *I did it for you.* "Jessie, try to understand."

"Oh, I understand perfectly. I didn't fit into your plans. Just as you don't fit into my plans now. We're colleagues, Gavin. And either we keep it at that, or I won't consult with you."

She'd not only gained in poise over the years, but in strength and confidence, too. "Jessie, I came to Four Oaks because of you. But if you want a strictly professional relationship, that's what we'll have. I think there's more, but you'll have to trust me enough to find out."

She took a few steps back. "Trust, Gavin? That's not a word I use lightly or easily."

There was so much about Jessica Windsor he'd never had the time to discover. But he would now. Even if the discovery had to be at a slower pace than he'd planned. He nodded to the folder on her desk.

"I'll call Rodney's parents and get back to you. We'll go from there."

He saw the relief in her eyes that he'd backed off. Almost too much relief. What had happened to her that she guarded herself so carefully? He vowed to himself he was going to find out.

A few days later, Jessie sat by her father's pool, trying to keep her mind on the magazine article she was reading. No matter how busy life seemed, she always tried to take Sunday afternoons to spend time with her father and Lisa. It had become a tradition Lisa looked forward to, a change from ordinary life. Instead of cleaning up after herself as Jessie had always insisted she do, here the maid took her empty glass to the kitchen and treated her like a little princess.

Thank goodness Lisa took it for what it was, an afternoon at Grandfather's, which was a bit different from the rest of ordinary life. She'd always loved the water and was now splashing around the shallow end of the pool.

Owen sat on the chair next to Jessie under the shade of the umbrella. Placing a stack of papers on the table beside him, he asked, "Have you seen Gavin Bradley yet?"

"We consulted about a patient." Ever since that kiss in her office, she didn't know what to do about Gavin. It had shaken her up so much, she was afraid to be around him, let alone tell him they had a daughter. "He said he wrote me a letter."

Her father shuffled through the papers on his pile. "You never received one. He must be lying."

"Unless it got lost."

Owen frowned. "I suppose that's possible."

"It really doesn't matter," Jessie reminded herself. She'd looked at Gavin's abandonment in the same way she'd looked at her mother's. Neither had wanted an attachment to her. They'd wanted to be free to live the life they wanted. And something deep inside of her had always told her something was wrong with her because she couldn't hold on to love. She'd thought she'd relegated all those insecurities to the past . . . until she'd seen Gavin again . . . until he'd kissed her.

She hadn't stuttered in years. But after Gavin's kiss, when her emotions were in such a swirl she could hardly see straight, words had almost stuck on her tongue. She'd used breathing and pauses and rehearsing the words in her mind as she always had, but she'd been so close to tripping up. She'd felt the unsureness that had been so much a part of her as a child.

Always, in the back of her mind, she remembered the whispers behind her back. She remembered teachers telling her father that she was a bright child, and as soon as she developed self-confidence, she would grow out of the stuttering. But she hadn't. Because she did well on written tests and schoolwork, her teachers didn't embarrass her by calling on her in class.

When she was in fifth grade, everyone in the class had been given an assignment for an oral presentation—except her. The teacher had told her that she could simply turn in a written report. Jessie had gone home in tears. When her father had asked her what was wrong, Jessie finally admitted, "I...d-d-don't want t-t-to b-be d-different."

The next day, her father called specialists in Roanoke. The day of her first appointment, Jessie started on the road to self-confidence because of a caring therapist who specialized in working with elementary-aged children. They were often the most difficult group to help because they'd developed patterns and habits that had become ingrained, and they usually lacked motivation to change their speech patterns—because learning not to stutter required work. But Jessie had been ready for the work, ready to change anything she could to become "normal," so her father would love her and she could be just like other kids her age.

Step by step, Jessie had learned how to speak fluently. The therapist understood Jessie's pain, embarrassment and frustration. Jessie had decided then and there that she wanted to do the same someday for children who were like her.

But for those moments after Gavin kissed her, she'd felt like her younger self, the one who'd stumbled over many words, unable to express herself. She knew automatically when she was upset or excited that she had to manage her breathing, speak slowly and pay attention to the way she articulated. But when Gavin's gray gaze had caught and held hers, she'd almost forgotten everything that had become second nature for years. She'd never told Gavin about her childhood problem. She'd intended to, but then . . .

Her father's words brought her back to the present. "You've established a good life, Jessica. I'd hate to see you disrupt it."

"I have to decide what's best for Lisa. Whenever she's asked about her father, I've told her he left before she was born. But she doesn't understand. She can't understand why she doesn't have a father like other children."

"You could have given her a father. I've introduced you to several suitable men. But you won't go out with them."

"You and I have never agreed on what 'suitable' was. But that's beside the point."

"What is the point? You want to give Gavin Bradley a second chance to hurt you? His kind—" Owen stopped abruptly.

"What do you mean 'his kind'? I never told you much about him."

"He left you high and dry before. So now he's a doctor. He'll never have time for you or his daughter. . . even if he stays in Four Oaks. Doctors are married to their profession. You know that. You're around them quite a bit."

Jessie knew her father was trying to protect her, and what he was saying was probably true. Gavin had been single-minded about becoming a doctor, which had included leaving her behind. Now that he was one, he would be just as single-minded. Still, didn't Lisa deserve to know her father?

*And what if he rejects her? Will she feel insecure
the rest of her life?*

Lisa mounted the steps of the pool, wrapped her
arms around herself and came to stand beside Jessie.
"Mommy, I don't feel good."

Jessie immediately flipped the magazine to the
ground, picked up a towel and wrapped it around her
daughter, who was shivering. "What's wrong,
honey?"

Her teeth were chattering although the temperature on this Sunday in May was at least eighty-five in
the sun. "My ear hurts and I'm cold."

Jessie stood and took Lisa's hand. "Come on. Let's
get you into dry clothes."

"Then what?" Owen Windsor asked.

Lisa had had earaches before, and only one thing
usually helped—an antibiotic. "Probably a trip to the
emergency room. I'll let you know before we leave."

A half hour later, Jessie sat beside her daughter on
the examining-room table. The nurse had pulled the
curtain around the small cubicle. Lisa nestled into her
mother's shoulder. Jessie stroked her hair and kissed
her forehead.

Suddenly Jessie heard footsteps, and a hand swept
the curtain aside. She looked up, saw the white coat,
and then . . . clear gray eyes.

Gavin.

Her arm tightened around her daughter, and she
waited for the bomb to explode.

Chapter Two

Gavin looked as surprised as Jessie felt. "They knew I was in pediatrics and paged me when the doctor in ER was tied up." He glanced at the form on the clipboard, and a strange expression crossed his face.

Coming into the cubicle, he stopped in front of Lisa. "Hi, there. My name's Dr. Bradley. What's yours?"

"Lisa." The eight-year-old sat up straight.

"Does something hurt today?" Gavin asked her.

She smiled timidly at Gavin's kind tone. "Uh-huh. My ear. It hurts a lot."

"When did it start?"

"At lunch."

"Honey, why didn't you tell me?" Jessie asked, focusing on her daughter rather than on what Gavin might learn from this visit.

"I wanted to go swimming."

Gavin gave a wry smile then said to Lisa, "I'm going to do a little examination." His gaze found Jessie's. "Lisa is eight?"

Jessie knew Lisa's birthdate was on the form on Gavin's clipboard. Her voice was hard to find, but she managed to say, "Yes."

His jaw tensed. Turning his back to her, he took a tongue depressor from a jar on the metal table.

Smiling a strained smile at Lisa, which Jessie suspected took quite a bit of effort, he said, "Let's look at your throat first, then I'll examine your ears. Give me the biggest 'Aaah' I've ever heard."

Lisa obliged.

Gavin then gently examined her ears, warmed his stethoscope and listened to her heart and lungs.

When he finished, he said to Jessie, "It's an ear infection, all right. I'll give you a prescription you can get filled at the hospital pharmacy." He ruffled Lisa's hair. "You should feel much better tomorrow. Make sure you tell your mom if you don't or if you feel dizzy. Ear infections can make you woozy, and I don't want you falling down stairs or anything like that. Your mom can help you get dressed, but then I want to see her outside alone for a few minutes."

Lisa looked worried. "So you can talk to her about me?"

"Yes, but it's nothing for you to worry about. Okay?"

Lisa studied him for a moment, then smiled and shook her head.

Jessie could tell Gavin had a wonderful way with children. He'd told Lisa exactly what he was going to do before he did it. And now he was reassuring her. Jessie could use some of that reassurance herself.

It seemed like forever until she got Lisa dressed and stepped outside the curtain. Gavin was waiting, his hands in the white lab-coat pockets, his stance rigid. In a low voice, he said, "We can't talk here, and I realize Lisa will need you tonight. Call me tomorrow to set up a time to meet. If you don't, I'll turn up on your doorstep. Understand?"

"Gavin, I never meant for you to find out this way."

"I wonder if you were going to tell me at all."

The anger in his voice put her on the defensive. "I have to make the right decisions for Lisa."

"So do I," he replied, his voice going deeper.

She could only imagine what he was feeling— shock, a sense of responsibility. Was there any joy that he had a daughter? Restricted by their surroundings, she couldn't ask.

"I'll be waiting for your call," he reminded curtly, then walked down the hall.

Tears pricked in Jessie's eyes, and she knew life was about to change for all of them. She just didn't know how much.

Tuesday morning, Jessie stood in front of Dr. Winnichuk's office, now Gavin's office, her palms sweaty, her heart beating in triple time. An X-ray technician Jessie knew smiled and nodded as she walked down the hospital corridor. Dr. Winnichuk had practiced from the hospital in Four Oaks since Jessie was a child. He'd always insisted he didn't need a fancy office on the outskirts of town, that being at the hospital was more economical and practical. And Peter Winnichuk still made house calls. The community would miss him if he retired.

Would Gavin take over his practice permanently? Now that he knew about Lisa . . .

Jessie opened the door and stepped over the threshold. She'd told Gavin she'd meet him as soon as she got Lisa off to school. When she entered the waiting area, she saw his receptionist hadn't yet arrived.

Jessie paced rather than sat. She'd figured meeting with Gavin here would be the safest. But when he opened the door to the waiting room and motioned her to follow him, she didn't feel safe.

She followed Gavin past examining rooms to his office. Inside, he arranged two chairs so they faced each other and motioned for her to sit.

After straightening her skirt over her knees, she met his gray eyes, her mouth going dry.

"Why didn't you let me know?"

Out of all the questions she'd guessed he'd ask, that wasn't the one she expected. "How was I supposed to let you know when I didn't even have your address?"

He wasn't moved by her outrage. "You could have contacted me through the university. They would have forwarded a letter to me."

She shifted in her chair, not wanting to bare her heart but not knowing how to avoid it. "Truthfully, Gavin, I didn't think you'd be interested."

"You were pregnant with my child," he said in a voice that was low with controlled vehemence.

"Yes, and I didn't think you'd care. You left me without a word. We made love, and you never called again. You tell me how I was *supposed* to feel. When I found out I was pregnant, I was scared. And confused. If it hadn't been for Dad..."

"He was supportive?" Gavin asked in a gentler voice.

"Once I convinced him I was keeping my baby. He wanted me to put her up for adoption. But I couldn't. He encouraged me to get my master's and he helped me the year after she was born."

Gavin raked his hand through his hair. "Jessie, I can see how it looked, especially if you never received my letter. But don't you think I deserved to know?"

Finally she glimpsed the pain behind the anger in his eyes. "I hadn't dated many men, Gavin. You were the first one who didn't push for sex right away. Many of my friends had one-night stands and never heard from the guys again."

He leaned forward in the chair, his knees brushing hers. "So you thought after I made love with you, that's all I wanted?"

Those gray eyes had always made her feel turned inside out, and today was no exception. "When you didn't call or write, what else was I supposed to think? And you can't tell me you would have been happy to learn I was pregnant. After all, Gavin, *you* broke it off."

"Jessie..."

She shook her head. "There's no point talking about the past, is there? I'm more concerned with the present."

Since Sunday afternoon, Gavin had thought about the past and the present. He'd asked himself *What if?* until it was a steady mantra that did absolutely no good. In a way, Jessie was right—the past didn't matter. But the passion and feelings from the past did because they influenced the present.

"You're scared of the feelings between us, aren't you?" he asked, noticing the tension in her shoulders, her hands clenched in her lap.

Her chin came up as she squared her shoulders. "No, I'm not scared. There are no feelings between us. They died a long time ago."

"What about the kiss, Jessie? You can't deny—"

"I can't deny you caught me off guard and I was once attracted to you. That's all it was, Gavin."

He looked at Jessie and wondered if she was right, if he was deluding himself thinking she might still care. But why hadn't she married? And why did she tremble when he touched her? There had always been a vulnerability about her. She'd learned to hide it, but he suspected it was still there.

Though he didn't want to, he might have to put aside, for the time being, the question of him and Jessie. "I'm Lisa's father and I want to be part of her life."

"For how long?" she asked, her concern for Lisa obvious.

"For always, Jessie. Now that I know about her, she's my responsibility as much as yours."

"What does that mean, Gavin? You can't just suddenly tell her you're her father and upset her whole world!"

"What does she know about me?" he asked calmly.

"She knows you left before she was born. That's it. I've pretended that you never existed, and you didn't, not for her. She's happy and well adjusted, and I want her to stay that way."

The pain of Jessie's words went deeper than any pain he'd ever known. "I want to see her, spend time with her and get to know her. I won't tell her I'm her father until you and I both decide the time is right. That's a promise."

Jessie appeared unsure.

"I won't hurt her," he vowed. He wanted to take Jessie's hand, make some kind of physical contact. But he knew if he moved forward, she'd back off. So he sat perfectly still and waited.

She brushed her hair behind her ear. "I need a few days to think about the best way to go about this. All right?"

He could nudge, but if he pushed he was afraid he'd lose them both. He took a card from the holder on his desk and wrote a number on the back. "That's my home phone. Call me when you decide. But don't wait too long, Jessie. I've already lost eight years."

Jessie stood then and went to the door. At the corridor, she paused. "I will call you, Gavin. I truly want what's best for our daughter."

Gavin felt his heart lighten just a little as Jessie left. She'd used the words *our daughter*. That was a beginning.

The next day Gavin's receptionist caught him between patients. "It's Jessica Windsor. You said to tell you immediately if she called."

"I'll take it in my office." He strode into the room at the end of the hall, shut the door and picked up the phone. "Hello, Jessie."

"I know you're busy...."

"Never too busy to talk to you about Lisa."

She was quiet for a few moments. "Our block is having a yard sale all day on Saturday and a covered dish picnic around five. If you want to spend some time around Lisa, it would be a good opportunity."

He wanted to spend time around Jessie, too. But if he told her that, she might withdraw the invitation. "Can I bring anything?"

"No. There will be plenty. I just hope it's a sunny day. Yard sales aren't fun in the rain."

"I've never been to a yard sale."

"Never?"

"Nope." In the neighborhood where he'd grown up, stealing was more popular than selling. "Maybe I can get there before it's over." When she didn't respond, he said, "Thanks for the invitation. This will be a good way to start."

"Gavin, I hope you don't expect too much. I hope..."

"I know I can't be Lisa's father overnight."

Jessie's silence told him she agreed. Finally she said, "I'll see you Saturday."

"Saturday," he repeated, and put down the receiver. Jessie didn't know what to expect, and to be truthful neither did he. Saturday would lay the groundwork.

The sun shown brightly on Saturday afternoon as Jessie packed up the odds and ends she hadn't sold at the yard sale. She'd enjoyed sitting with her neighbors while their children played not too far away. All winter Lisa had begged and begged Jessie for a skateboard. Reluctantly she'd given in. Now, with a helmet, arm and knee pads, her daughter rolled up and down the sidewalk in front of their house with her friends.

Jessie had begun watching for Gavin around four. But by five, when she started to pack up, he still hadn't arrived. After she carried the boxes to her garage, she went into the kitchen to ready the food they'd need for supper.

By six the neighbors sat in lawn chairs they'd carried to Jessie's patio. Casseroles and bowls of various sizes covered Jessie's picnic table. Lisa sat next to her mother, balancing her plate on her lap, and scooped up her last spoonful of baked beans. Suddenly she pointed to the side of the house. "There's Dr. Bradley!" She waved, set her plate in the grass and ran over to him.

As the minutes had ticked by after five o'clock, Jessie had found herself getting annoyed and then downright angry. She was glad she hadn't told Lisa that Gavin was coming.

But now Lisa stood beside him, all smiles, telling all her neighbors Dr. Bradley was her new doctor. Jessie looked at the two of them, studying their facial features. Lisa had Gavin's cheekbones and his thick black hair and lashes. They were a striking father and daughter.

Gavin came up to Jessie. "I'm sorry I'm late. I had an emergency."

He was dressed in casual slacks and a tan oxford shirt, his sleeves rolled up to his forearms. But on his feet he wore Reeboks! A man of the nineties, all right. He looked taller, sexier, and made her heart race faster each time she saw him. Annoyed with herself, she stood and dumped her plate and Lisa's into a trash bag. "I bet you have a lot of emergencies."

He clasped her elbow. "I'm a doctor, Jessie." The heat from his hand flashed up her arm.

She went still and met his probing gaze. "I know."

His voice low, he said, "I'm here now, but I am on call."

"Then I guess you'd better grab some food while you can." She knew her voice was crisp but couldn't help it. Several of her neighbors were watching her interchange with Gavin curiously.

"I want another hot dog," Lisa said, smiling up at him. She pointed next door. "We have to go over there to get them. Mrs. Donahue is making them on her grill."

Jessie gestured to the casseroles. "Most of the hot ones have gotten cold. I can heat some up in my microwave...."

He released her arm and shook his head. "Hot dogs will be fine. Don't go to any trouble."

Lisa took him by the hand. "Come on. Mrs. Donahue has plates over there."

Lisa showed Gavin the pasta salad that was her favorite and, after he'd eaten, insisted on getting him a piece of chocolate cake like hers. For the most part, Jessie just watched as her daughter chattered about her new skateboard, and her best friend, Marly, who was sitting three chairs away. As Gavin listened to his daughter, he also managed to make conversation with Jessie's next-door neighbor, Shannon Miller, Marly's mother, and her husband, Ted. Jessie couldn't believe how easily he fit in. It took *her* a while to make friends, to find her niche. But then it always had.

Finally tired of eating and sitting with the adults, Lisa and Marly scampered over to the swing set. Shannon stood and clapped her hands. "Volleyball, everyone. Let's work off that supper!"

She didn't let the groans and laughs dissuade her as she urged and nudged her neighbors from their chairs. Her dark brown hair pulled back in a ponytail swung over her shoulder as she took Jessie's hand and pulled her up. "Come on. You, too, Dr. Bradley."

"Gavin," he said with a smile.

"All right, Gavin. I'll put you and Jessie on the same team, and we'll see what you can do." She clapped her hands again. "Let's move it, everyone."

As Shannon and Ted crossed to the net, Gavin chuckled. "Is she a drill sergeant?"

Jessie couldn't suppress her smile. "Nope, but a darn good neighbor and friend. She and Ted have helped us feel at home in the development."

Gavin walked beside her, his arm brushing hers. "How long have you lived here?"

"Two years. I got tired of paying rent and having nothing to show for it."

"I'd like to invest in a house, finally get a real feeling of permanence."

"Where are you staying?"

"An apartment on Linden Avenue. It's the first floor of an older home, lots of space, a beautiful yard. You and Lisa will have to stop by."

"I have a feeling you won't be home very much," she said in a wry tone.

They'd almost reached the group at the net. Gavin stopped and blocked her from going forward. "Jessie, I'm a doctor. But I can still have a life. It just takes some flexibility."

She wasn't concerned for herself, just her daughter. "A life also takes time, Gavin. Do you have time for Lisa?"

He held Jessie by the shoulders and looked deep into her eyes. "Yes."

His gaze kept her trapped, and she couldn't look away.

Suddenly Shannon stood next to them, handing Jessie the volleyball. "You serve."

Jessie felt color creep up her neck. Shannon's gaze was much too knowing. She knew she was going to have some explaining to do when the evening was over. No one in Four Oaks knew about Gavin and her. No one but her father.

Jessie could feel Gavin's gaze on her throughout the game. Every once in a while, she'd steal a sideways glance at him. When he wasn't in play or watching her, his gaze followed his daughter as she ran and played with the other children.

Shannon and Ted often organized a volleyball game in their yard. Jessie found the sport good exercise and lots of fun. But Gavin playing in front of her or beside her or behind her changed her normally good serves into duds and her spikes into grounders.

Between rotations, Shannon murmured to her, "Relax, kid. He doesn't care how you play."

Embarrassed, Jessie was more determined than ever to play up to par. Gavin certainly was. He'd scored point after point for their team.

The other side served. Jessie flexed her knees, readying herself, waiting for her chance. Gavin was somewhere behind her, and for the moment she tried to block out his presence.

Shannon popped up the serve with both hands. It flew over the net. The other side lobbed it back. The ball soared high over the first line. Jessie stepped back, back, back, her arms raised and as the ball came down, she heard her name, reached higher and collided with someone tall and hard. Strong arms came around her to steady her. She saw the forearms with curling black hair, the rolled-up shirtsleeves, and took a deep breath of hot male.

Gavin.

As she stood with her back pressed against his stomach and chest, everything about him was so familiar she ached.

He murmured in her ear, "We lost it." Nudging her around, he asked, "Are you okay?"

No, she wasn't okay. She'd lost her breath and all her senses. She wanted him to kiss her, right here, right now, and didn't care who watched. She must be crazy!

Gavin saw the longing in Jessie's eyes. He recognized it because he felt it, too. But after the way she'd reacted in her office, he knew he had to proceed carefully.

Pulling away, restraining the urge to keep his arm curled around her waist, he said over his shoulder to the others, "We're going to take a break."

"Gavin, we can't," Jessie protested. "We're in the middle of a game!"

He urged her toward the house. "Some things are definitely more important than others. They'll survive without us."

The patio was empty, though the children were within shouting distance. It took Gavin all of his self-control not to touch Jessie, not to take her in his arms as he'd longed to for years. The thought of Jessie, the memory of her smile, her soft voice, her loving, had gotten him through thirty-six-hour shifts, endless odd jobs, scrimping the past two years to make a dent in his loans. But now he was on his way. They had a daughter together and, he hoped, a lot more.

"If you look at me again like you did out there, I'm going to kiss you. I'm giving fair warning," he scolded.

The pulse at her throat beat rapidly. "Why are you telling me?"

"Because we need honesty between us, Jessie. That's the only way we'll get to trust. I want to kiss you. And I want you to be honest enough to admit that you want it, too."

Her blue eyes, usually so clear and bright, became shadowed. "Just because I want something doesn't mean I should have it or take it or give it. What I want and what's best are two different things. The truth is, Gavin—I don't know if I can ever trust you again."

He felt as if he'd taken a belt to the jaw. He could see she wasn't just stringing words together to hurt him. The anguish on her face was as deep as what he felt.

She shifted away from him and stared at Lisa. "You really don't know very much about me, Gavin."

He clasped her shoulder and urged her toward him again. "I know I cared about you deeply once. And you cared about me."

"And then you left me. How can I believe you won't do it again? To Lisa? Freedom is an odd thing. It's much more of a lure to some people than others."

When he'd made plans to return to Four Oaks, had he thought winning Jessie back would be easy? No, but he'd never expected what he had found, either— a daughter, and Jessie fighting against everything they'd once felt for each other. They'd have to start over. They'd have to...

His pager beeped.

All Gavin's life, he'd dreamed of being a doctor. He'd held on to that dream when rats ran across the floor of their tenement, when his drunken father had yelled and screamed that he'd never amount to anything, when his mother died because of the lack of good medical care. He'd never minded answering a page because he was doing exactly what he wanted to do.

But right now he swore with frustration because he saw Jessie's face register her dismay that once again his career was calling him away.

"Can I use your phone?"

She left his side and opened the storm door, flipping on the light over the counter.

His quick look around told him she liked a homey kitchen. Blue gingham curtains graced the window over the sink. The material also covered her toaster and mixer. Matching pot holders hung on the side of the refrigerator, along with magnets of all shapes and sizes that held pictures Lisa had drawn.

The smell of baked beans still lingered in the air as he went to the phone.

Jessie quietly cleaned up the debris from the picnic. Opening the dishwasher, she transferred dishes and silverware from the sink, wondering if she and Gavin would ever be able to finish a conversation without his pager going off.

A few minutes later, Gavin hung up the phone. "I have to get to the hospital. One of my patients is spiking a temp of 104 degrees.'' He strode to the door. ''I'll say goodbye to Lisa on my way out.''

Jessie stayed at the counter.

''I'll call you.''

She nodded.

He scowled. ''Don't look at me like that. I said I'll call you and I will.''

Gavin had always been able to read her thoughts too well. ''I understand, Gavin.''

He swore and reached her in two long strides. Without warning, he pulled her into his arms, kissed her with a demanding force that made her grab his shoulders, then he set her away and murmured, ''I'm not sure you understand at all. But you will.''

Before her breathing returned to normal, he was gone. She sagged against the counter and pressed her fingers to her lips. Everything about Gavin Bradley packed a wallop. She just had to make sure she safeguarded her balance, her bearings and her heart—for her sake, as well as her daughter's.

Chapter Three

The light of a full moon streamed in through Jessie's bedroom window as she closed it partway before turning in. She loved the spring air and didn't want to shut it out altogether.

She was just about to get under the bed covers when the phone rang. Jumping in surprise, she snatched up the receiver and checked the time on her digital clock—11:00 p.m. Seating herself on the edge of the bed, she said, "Hello?"

"Jessie. Did I wake you?"

She closed her eyes against the effect of Gavin's voice. "No. I'd just turned out the light."

Gavin paused for a moment. "Are you in bed now?" he asked, his voice husky.

"On it, not in it." Suddenly she vividly remembered the night she'd spent with Gavin in his bed. Taking a deep breath, she tried to block it out.

"I just finished at the hospital or I wouldn't have called so late. Are you and Lisa busy tomorrow?"

"We usually go to Dad's for lunch and swimming in the afternoon."

"I want to see you and Lisa again. I'm painting my living room tomorrow and I wondered if the two of you would like to help. I have to make rounds in the morning, but we could start about two, maybe order a pizza for supper."

She went to her father's every Sunday. Not going one week wouldn't hurt. If Lisa was going to get to know Gavin, she needed to spend time with him. "All right. I can call Dad in the morning."

"Does he know you told me about Lisa?"

"No."

"You'll tell him tomorrow?"

"Probably."

"Jessie, I'm not going to go away, so he might as well get used to me being around."

There was a determination in Gavin's voice that unnerved her. Maybe she did hope he'd go away. *Or maybe you* expect *him to go away. Again.*

"What time did everyone leave tonight?"

She had to switch gears. Remembering the picnic, the volleyball game, Gavin holding her when they'd collided, his kiss, she answered, "Around nine. Lisa was beat. She didn't even argue about going to bed as she usually does."

"She's a terrific little girl. You've done a great job."

"Loving her has never been a chore. But she has more energy than a whirlwind. I don't think you realize what you're doing asking her to help paint. Are you sure about this?"

"Very sure. I don't want to be the kind of father who just takes her to the circus or the movies. I want everyday life with her. Painting should be fun."

An everyday father. Exactly what did that mean for her and Gavin, as well as for Lisa?

"Jessie?"

"Yes?"

"I'm looking forward to tomorrow."

"Gavin, don't expect too much. Don't expect—"

"I'm not expecting anything except getting my living room painted in the company of two lovely ladies. I won't keep you up. Good night, Jessie. Sweet dreams."

"Good night." Jessie put the phone on its cradle slowly. She felt as if she'd stepped aboard a runaway train and didn't know how to get off. All she could do was to keep applying the brakes and hope she could slow down. Nine years ago, she'd enjoyed the excitement of the ride and had crashed. She wasn't about to be that foolish again.

As Jessie drove to Gavin's apartment, she thought about her conversation with her father. He'd been strangely silent when she told him Gavin knew Lisa was his daughter. Owen Windsor was rarely silent about anything.

Lisa was eager to visit Gavin and asked Jessie, "What's the number?"

"It's 2701. We should almost be there...."

Lisa pointed to a stately two-story home surrounded by tall maples. "There it is. It doesn't look like an apartment!"

No, it didn't, with its long double windows, red-brick exterior and black shutters; it looked like a single-family dwelling.

Jessie pulled up to the curb and hardly had time to switch off the ignition before Lisa opened her door. As she hopped out, Jessie called, "Wait a minute."

Lisa flung over her shoulder, "I want to ring the bell," and kept going.

Jessie's heart beat faster as she thought about seeing Gavin again. She hurried after her daughter, trying to stay calm. But when she reached the porch where her daughter stood and the door opened, the butterflies in her stomach fluttered their wings with renewed vigor.

There should be a law against a man looking that sexy in a T-shirt and jeans—faded, well-worn jeans that fit snugly enough to tempt Jessie to look where she shouldn't.

He stepped back into the foyer and motioned them inside. "Just in time to stir the paint." He tweaked Lisa's ponytail.

"I never painted before," Lisa said. "Except for finger paints."

"I'll teach you everything you need to know," he offered with a grin for his daughter. "As long as your mom doesn't mind you getting some paint on you and your clothes.''

"We wore old clothes," Lisa assured him. "If I get some on me, will it wash off?"

A stairway led up to what Jessie presumed was the second-floor apartment. Gavin opened a door to the right, which led into his living space on the first floor. Lisa scurried by him, eager to see. Jessie followed more slowly. As she passed Gavin, her arm brushed his stomach. It was as hard and taut as he was fit. Her gaze shot up to his. Neither of them breathed.

The flash of desire in his eyes scared her, and she quickly moved into the living room. Sheets covered a sofa and chair. There was no other furniture.

Gavin came closer to Jessie and answered his daughter's question. "The paint is water based, so it will wash off."

Lisa scurried over to an open can and peered into it. "That's a pretty color. Mom, see?"

The shade was pale green—light and comfortable. Trying to ignore the tingling awareness of Gavin a few feet away from her, Jessie stared at the walls, a depressing taupe color with black marks and crayon streaks marring it to eye level. "No wonder your landlord is letting you paint."

"You should have seen the kids' bedroom. It took me a day just to scrub the walls."

Jessie laid her purse on the sheet-covered chair. "Well, let's get started. Do you have buckets and detergent?"

"In the kitchen. It's the only room that's completely habitable."

"You're sleeping on the sofa?"

He chuckled. "No. I do have a bed, but that's it. Maybe you'd like to go furniture and accessory shopping sometime?"

He was trying to draw her into his life. Fear made her cautious. "We'll see."

"Dr. Bradley, can I stir this now?" Lisa asked, already impatient with standing still.

Gavin switched his attention to his daughter and crouched down beside her. He nodded to the wooden stirring sticks lying on the newspaper beside the paint can. "Use one of those and go around in a circle at the edges of the can. The secret is to do it slowly so it doesn't spill out all over."

Lisa picked up the stick, dipped it into the paint and gave Gavin a huge smile.

Jessie watched the expression on Gavin's face. It was proud and filled with fatherly satisfaction. Even if her feelings for Gavin had died, she couldn't keep him from his daughter.

Gavin stood and beckoned to Jessie to follow him.

The kitchen also glowed with a coat of new white paint. Knotty-pine-paneled cabinets hung across one wall. Beige Formica topped the bottom cupboards. A round, dark pine table and two chairs sat in a small alcove.

"You found a lovely apartment," she commented, nervous being alone with him in the small kitchen.

"I'm not sure what to do with it. The kitchen seems a little bland, don't you think?"

Before she could catch herself, she suggested, "A colorful wallpaper border near the ceiling might work."

"I like that idea." He took a bucket from under the sink, poured dishwashing detergent into it and filled it. Turning off the spigot, he asked, "How did your father deal with your canceling your plans with him?"

"He didn't say much."

"How did you feel about what he didn't say?" Gavin asked with a sideways glance at her.

She sighed. "As if I'm doing something he doesn't approve of. But I'm used to that."

"What do you mean?"

"He wasn't happy when Lisa and I moved out of his house. He's constantly suggesting we move back. I think he hopes I won't be able to keep up mortgage payments on the town house so I'll reconsider."

Gavin lifted the bucket from the sink. "What are the chances of that happening?"

"As long as I do my job and do it well, it won't. But Dad can always hope, I guess."

"Certainly he wants to see you succeed."

"I suppose he does. But he also wants to keep me under his thumb. I keep slipping out."

Gavin's lips twitched up at that. "You've grown up, Jessie."

"I had to. And I had to do it fast for Lisa's sake."

He set the bucket on the counter and came closer. "She comes first, doesn't she?"

The light in Gavin's eyes, his male scent, vivid memories, made Jessie swallow hard before she answered, "Always."

Gavin cocked his head. "And does your father come second?"

"What do you mean?"

"You don't like his disapproval."

"No, I don't."

"What happens if your father opposes me spending time with Lisa?"

Gavin's intense gray gaze said he expected a straight answer. Searching her heart, Jessie said honestly, "I'll do what's best for Lisa."

"Do I have your word on that?"

"Gavin, why are you pushing so hard? I have to take one day at a time...."

He stepped even closer and held her by the shoulders. "I've missed eight years of my daughter's life. I don't intend to lose any more, no matter what your father thinks."

"Shh," Jessie warned. "I don't want her to hear you."

"I think we should tell her."

"No!"

Gavin frowned. "I won't hurt her, Jessie."

"I don't know that. Don't you see I have to protect her?"

"Like your father protected you?"

"I don't know what you mean."

From Jessie's expression, Gavin could see that she didn't. If Owen Windsor had manipulated her life once, Gavin suspected that wasn't the only time. Yet he also knew if he drove a wedge between Jessie and her father, he'd probably also drive another wedge between Jessie and himself. It was obvious she loved her father. Telling her about Owen's visit, relaying his suspicion that Owen might have intercepted the letter, wouldn't change anything. She felt as if Gavin had abandoned her, and all the noblest reasons in the world wouldn't change that.

"Maybe I know what's best for Lisa as well as you do. Maybe I can be more objective than you or your father where Lisa is concerned."

She pulled away from him. "Now, wait a minute. Don't think you can barge into our lives and turn everything upside down. I won't let you."

He stuffed his hands into his pockets to keep from yanking her into his arms. He'd dreamed of her too many nights not to want to put some of those dreams into action. "I have rights where Lisa in concerned. Being her father gives me those rights," he added, his voice low but vehement. "If you had bothered to inform me we had a child, I would have claimed them sooner!" Suddenly he realized how angry he was with Jessie that he'd lost those years with his daughter.

"Maybe my father was right. Maybe I shouldn't have told you," Jessie concluded, her voice shaking.

"You *didn't* tell me. I found out by accident," he countered, not wanting to admit how much that hurt.

Jessie opened her mouth but then shut it again as if she'd thought about what she wanted to say and decided it wasn't a good idea.

"What?" he asked impatiently.

"Nothing."

He shook his head. "Don't give me that. Tell me what you're thinking so I know what I'm up against."

He saw her muster her courage and knew she was going to give it to him with both barrels. "All right. I'll tell you. I don't think you have any idea how your arrival in Four Oaks is affecting my life. From the moment I heard you were coming here, I couldn't stop the rush of painful memories. I remembered how used I felt after graduation when you didn't call. I remembered going through my pregnancy, lonely, wishing for support. I remembered explaining I was having a baby and I wasn't married. That's not something men have to worry too much about."

"Jessie . . ."

"No. Let me finish. You said you wanted to know what I was thinking."

"Go ahead," Gavin said reluctantly, knowing he'd asked for this.

She crossed her arms over her chest as if to barricade her heart. "Most of all, from the moment I knew you were coming, I was afraid. Afraid you'd find out about Lisa. Afraid if you did, our lives would never be the same. I've worked hard to be a good mother, to build my career so Lisa and I would have some security. And now you want to butt in and tell me you can do better. I'm thinking now maybe my fears are justified." Swiveling around, she went to the counter and picked up the bucket. "We'll help you paint your walls, Gavin, but I'm still not sure I want to invite you into my life."

With that, Jessie carried the bucket to his living room, her back straight, her shoulders square.

He'd asked what he was up against and now he knew. So where in the hell did he go from here?

Gavin watched as Jessie vigorously scrubbed the marks on the wall. He knew she was taking out her frustration on it rather than him. For the time being, he'd let her. Only time would show her he was here to stay, that she could trust him to want and do what was best for her and Lisa.

He helped his daughter get situated with a brush and paint in a corner. With plastic sheets covering the carpet, he told her not to worry about drips, then began to paint the wall along the baseboard and door frames.

A few minutes later he watched Jessie as she stopped her scrubbing and positioned the ladder in a corner. With expertise that told him she'd done this before, she poured some paint into one of the trays and carefully placed it on the step ladder's paint shelf.

Moving toward her, Gavin grabbed the ladder and held it steady while she climbed up.

Brush in hand, she looked down at him. "I'm fine. I painted our town house, so I know what I'm doing."

"I'm not questioning your ability, Jessie. But I'm not sure this ladder is too steady."

"I'm fine, Gavin."

She was one independent lady, and he knew he was going to have to give her some space. He let go of the ladder. "Give a yell if you need help."

Ignoring him, Jessie dipped her brush in the paint and stroked along the ceiling.

"Dr. Bradley, look. I'm all done this corner," Lisa said proudly.

Crossing the room, Gavin examined his daughter's work. "You did an excellent job. Let's move you to another corner. How would you like to paint to music? I can bring out my radio from the bedroom."

"Cool!" Lisa said. "Mom likes to sing along. Don't you?"

"Not when I have an audience," she murmured.

"Dr. Bradley's not an audience. I'll bet he'd like to hear you sing. She has a pretty voice," Lisa assured him.

Gavin suppressed a grin at Jessie's chagrin. "I bet she does."

And so the afternoon went, with the radio playing top-forty hits, Lisa chattering to him about everything from school to her escapades with Marly on their skateboards. Jessie hummed along softly to the music when she forgot herself.

When Lisa got bored, Gavin let her roll paint on the wall. Using two hands, she did her darnedest to paint just as he did. Suddenly she pointed to her arms and giggled. "I've got speckles all over me!"

Gavin chuckled. "I'm afraid I see a few in your hair, too."

Lisa looked up at her mother.

"Don't worry about it, honey. I have them, too. We'll clean up when we get home."

Lisa put down her roller. "My arms are tired. Can I go get my books in the car?"

Jessie started down the ladder. "Let me help you wash up first, or you'll get paint . . ."

Gavin saw Jessie's sneaker catch on the rung and the ladder wobble. He caught her around the waist as the paint tray flipped over and fell onto the plastic covering the carpet.

Jessie's backside pressed against his thigh as he continued holding her around the waist. "Are you okay?"

She looked over her shoulder, and while she gripped his forearms, their eyes met. They were a man and woman, severely aware of their bodies pressed close together, aware of their past history, the attraction they were fighting now. More than anything, Gavin wanted to turn Jessie around and kiss her senseless. But their daughter was watching. And he didn't want to push Jessie further away.

She loosened her grip and said in a whisper, "I'm fine."

Her hair brushed his cheek as he raised his head and let go of her waist.

Lisa stared at the paint tray. "What a mess!"

Jessie pushed her hair behind her ear, and Gavin felt her take a deep breath. "I'll get the paper towels."

Gavin didn't want to take his hands from her or let her go, but he had no choice. "I have a spare roll under the sink in the kitchen, Lisa. Will you go get it?"

She nodded and scampered off.

Jessie turned then and faced him. "I'm really sorry about the mess. If I had been more careful . . ."

"We both should have been more careful." Suddenly they weren't discussing spilled paint.

Her voice softened. "We were young."

"And foolish."

Jessie hesitated a moment, then asked, "What's the real reason you didn't call or write?"

Obviously she was still trying to make sense of it. Maybe it wasn't too late. "I had nothing to offer you, Jessie."

Her eyes filled with sadness. "That's not true. If we had feelings for each other, we could have nurtured them. I would have waited. I could have helped...."

"That's exactly what I didn't want," he said, old hurts rising up, making his voice almost sharp.

She shook her head. "That's the problem. Our future was determined by what *you* wanted. And you might want to get to know Lisa now, but that doesn't mean you'll want a relationship with her a year from now."

"At some point, you'll have to trust me."

"I don't trust anyone but myself, Gavin. I haven't since I learned I was pregnant. I can't take the risk."

"You don't trust your father?"

"He has his own agenda."

"You must be very lonely," Gavin said gently.

She raised her chin, and her blue eyes became shuttered. "I'm not lonely. I have Lisa."

"Children are only part of the picture, Jessie."

Before she could respond, Lisa came running in with the paper towels. "Who's gonna start?"

Gavin took the roll from her, then glanced at Jessie. "We can all work on it together."

Taking a break from Gavin's disturbing presence, Jessie went into the kitchen to wash her hands. While they were in the same room, she couldn't keep her gaze from Gavin. She couldn't help looking and wondering and waiting. And she didn't even know what she was waiting for. His probing gray eyes unnerved her. His broad shoulders and muscular arms disturbed her. His deep voice, coaxing—and gentle yet determined, too—disconcerted her.

She looked at him and she hurt. She remembered the feelings she had once had. But even stronger was the sense of betrayal she'd experienced with his silence. He acted as if nine years was two months. He acted as if he'd made the right decision. But his choice had been wrong, and she didn't think she'd ever be able to erase the pain. Gavin was one of the reasons she didn't trust easily. Her mother's abandonment had shaken the foundations of her childhood, and Gavin's abandonment had toppled her illusions about loving and trusting as an adult.

So how could she ever put her well-being or Lisa's in his hands?

Flipping off the spigot, she reached for the towel hanging over the oven handle. Before she'd finished drying her hands, Gavin appeared, Lisa not far behind.

He carried a huge white box. "I thought we could eat under the tree out back and get out of here for a while."

The paint was a new kind that didn't have much odor, but it was still paint. "That sounds good. What do we need?"

He nodded to the cabinet above the sink. "There are paper plates up there. I'll get the soda. There's a blanket on the back porch."

"I'll spread out the blanket," Lisa offered, pushing open the screen door and jumping from the step.

He smiled. "She can't stand still, can she?"

"Not for any length of time. She wanted to bring her skateboard along, but I wasn't sure if you had pavement and I don't want her in the street."

"Lord, no!"

"She sees other kids doing it and thinks she should be able to. Peer pressure's already tough."

Gavin frowned. "Peer pressure's tough at any age. Kids want to be all the same. They hate to stand out for any reason."

How well she knew that! Her stuttering had set her painfully apart from the others. Gavin, too, sounded as if he'd had firsthand experience with peer disapproval. But before she could ask him about it, he'd gathered the cans of soda and walked to the door.

"Let's get to the pizza before it gets cold." Opening the door with his elbow, he held it until she stepped onto the porch.

Lisa was already sitting under a maple tree, the blanket spread around her. Gavin set the pizza box in front of her and sat.

Jessie positioned herself cross-legged beside her daughter, then opened the box. She slipped a slice of pizza onto a plate for Lisa.

"This is neat. I like your yard, Dr. Bradley. Did you plant the flowers?" Lisa asked, then took a bite of pizza.

He glanced at the bed of tulips, the fuchsia azaleas along the fence bordered by candytuft. "No. My neighbor upstairs likes to garden."

"Is she older?" Jessie asked, suddenly curious about who lived above him.

"No, she's about our age. You probably know her. Patricia Rogers. She's the personnel and special-programs director at the hospital. She's the one who recommended this apartment."

Jessie had a nodding acquaintance with Patti Rogers. The woman was an attractive blonde with a pleasant personality. "I don't know Patti well."

"She's very nice. Helpful."

"I'll just bet," Jessie muttered, knowing most women would be attracted to Gavin's dark good looks. She took a slice of pizza for herself, although her hunger had suddenly diminished.

Gavin helped himself to a piece of pizza. When she glanced at him, she caught an amused twinkle in his eyes. He probably thought she was jealous. Well, he could just think again.

"Hey, Mom. We pick up my outfit for the recital tomorrow, don't we?"

"I'll stop for it on my way home from work."

"What kind of recital are you in?" Gavin asked.

"Ballet. It's really cool! I'm this flower. There's lots of other flowers, too. And trees and ladybugs."

Before Lisa could invite Gavin to the recital and create an awkward situation with her grandfather, who would also be there, Jessie said, "After we finish the pizza, you could study your spelling words. You have a test tomorrow, remember?"

Lisa frowned. "I know."

"You can sit on my bed if you'd like," Gavin suggested.

Lisa's blue eyes sparkled. "I saw it. It's a *big* bed."

"King-size." He knocked his sneakers together. "So my feet don't hang out."

Lisa giggled.

But when Jessie reached for her soda and her eyes collided with Gavin's, her mind created much different images than his feet hanging over the footboard. And from the darkening gray of his eyes, she knew he knew it.

A short time later, as Lisa settled in Gavin's bedroom, Jessie picked up the smaller paintbrush to use on the baseboard.

Gavin started on the door frame.

Without the radio blaring, without Lisa's chattering, Jessie was aware of much more than the silence between her and Gavin. She felt like a college student with him again—gauche, unsure of herself, almost tongue-tied. His confidence and determination had attracted her to him years ago. He was even more self-assured now, and along with his sex appeal, she found the combination potent and all too disruptive to her peace of mind.

A breeze blew through the living room, and as dusk fell, Gavin switched on the overhead light. He disappeared for a few moments and, when he came back, he was smiling. "She ran out of steam. She's asleep."

Jessie shook her head. "She was up at the crack of dawn, all excited about coming over today."

His smile faded. "I was up at the crack of dawn, too. For the same reason."

His honesty touched Jessie. She laid her brush across the corner of the paint tray. "She likes you, Gavin. Anyone could see that."

He crouched down beside her. "Anyone?"

She gazed into his clear gray eyes. "*I* can see that."

Gavin knelt beside her and lifted her chin. "Thank you for coming today. I know you have reservations."

She tried to duck her head, but he wouldn't let her.

"Jessie, stop fighting it," he coaxed, his hands moving to her shoulders to pull her up to him.

She didn't know whether to give in or run. But she couldn't run. Not with Gavin sliding his hand under her hair. Not with Gavin lifting her chin so gently and lowering his head so slowly...

Chapter Four

Gavin planned to win Jessie again, degree by degree, slowly, so she wouldn't have any doubts. But each time he got a little too close, he wanted fast, not slow. Jessie had always done that to him.

Kneeling with her now, her blue eyes so wide and vulnerable, the scent of her shampoo enticing him closer, her pink lips soft and inviting, there was no way he could pull back or deny the chemistry between them. His hand slid under her hair, and he tilted her head. Nothing could have kept him from setting his lips on hers.

She made a soft sound in her throat when their lips met. Aroused, encouraged that she wanted this as much as he did, he slid his tongue along the seam of her lips. She opened to him and held on to his shoulders.

Giving in to temptation, he thrust his tongue into her mouth, possessing her with long, deep strokes that told her how much he'd missed her, how long he'd waited to find this passion again. Her hands grazed his neck and laced in his hair. Her touch was as arousing as he'd remembered.

Time, surroundings and caution forgotten, he took her down with him onto the plastic. He needed more than a kiss. He wanted to touch Jessie and know her again. Caressing her back, he drew her tighter against him. She slipped her hand under his arm and clutched his shirt. With a groan, he cupped her buttocks and rocked against her. When he shifted to move his leg between hers, his foot hit the paint tray and it rattled.

Abruptly Jessie broke the kiss. "No. I can't do this. I can't." She looked mortified, aroused and anguished all at the same time.

He wanted to cuddle her and tell her everything would be all right. "Jessie, you know there has always been this chemistry between us."

She sat up and straightened her top. "That doesn't mean we have to act on it. Gavin, it's been nine years!"

"And everything's the same when I kiss you, isn't it?"

"You don't know me anymore, Gavin, and I don't know you."

"I know you love our daughter."

She shook her head. "That's not enough."

"Then let me get to know you again. Give us time together, as well as time for me and Lisa. Give us a second chance, Jessie."

Her eyes were wide with doubts. "I don't know if I want to let you get close again. I don't know if I can."

"Are you willing to try?" Lisa couldn't be the only bond. He wanted much more than that.

"I need time to think about it."

At his frown, she continued, "Gavin, you came to Four Oaks expecting to see me, but I never expected to see you again. I thought you were gone from my life."

He rose to his feet and offered her his hand. When she took it, he tugged her up. "You think about it." He gently traced her upper lip with his finger. "While you're thinking, try to remember the fun we had, as well as the passion. And most of all, remember I left because I thought that's what was best for you."

Tipping her chin up, he tenderly kissed her lips. When he broke away, he saw all the doubts were still there. He'd give her time and he'd show her he wasn't going anywhere. Right now Jessie needed actions more than she needed words.

"You go wake Lisa. She has school tomorrow. I know you want to get her home."

"But we didn't finish—"

"I'll finish it. It won't take long."

Jessie hesitated for a moment, then went down the hall to Gavin's bedroom.

He would convince her the past wasn't just a memory. He would convince her the future could be theirs.

Monday evening, Jessie was emptying the dishwasher when her neighbor Shannon rapped on the back door.

"C'mon in," Jessie called as she lifted the cereal bowls to the top cabinet.

Shannon came in, pulled out a kitchen chair and parked there as if she was very much at home. "I wanted to know how you like Lisa's costume."

Jessie had to smile. She admired Shannon for her ability to seem at ease everywhere. "She's putting it on now. In fact—"

Before she could finish, her daughter bounded into the kitchen and pirouetted in front of them in her green tights and a pink tutu. "What do you think, Mom?"

Jessie exchanged a look with Shannon and smiled. "I think you look like a ballerina."

Lisa pirouetted two more times, finally bumping into a kitchen chair. She collapsed onto it with a giggle. "Hi, Mrs. Miller. Won't Marly and I look cool?"

Shannon said seriously, "The coolest. Maybe your mom and I should get outfits like that so we look cool, too."

"Nah. You'd look funny as flowers. You're grown-ups!"

Shannon bit back a smile. "So much for cool."

"Mom, you know what I really want?" Lisa asked.

Jessie closed the dishwasher. "What?"

"I want Dr. Bradley to come to my recital. Will you ask him?"

Jessie sighed. "Dr. Bradley's very busy, honey."

"But you can ask, can't you?"

Jessie rarely said no to her daughter if she could help it, unless it was a matter of discipline or safety. But Jessie needed some time to accept Gavin into their lives and decide if she wanted him in hers, as well as Lisa's. She didn't want to be pushed into it by Gavin or Lisa.

"Not this time, honey. Grandfather and I will be there. You can perform for us this time."

"Mom..."

"That's it. Subject closed. Do you need any help getting out of that?"

Lisa pointed her toes and looked down at her green ballet slippers. "Nope. I can do it. Mom, are you sure...?"

"I'm sure."

"When are we going to see Dr. Bradley again?"

"I don't know. Now go on up and get ready for bed. Give a shout when you're ready."

Lisa mumbled, "Okay," and left the kitchen with a lot less energy than when she'd come in.

"What's going on, Jessie?" Shannon asked. "You usually talk everything out with Lisa instead of coming down like the all-knowing parent."

Shannon had been a good friend ever since Jessie and Lisa had moved into the town house. They trusted each other with their children and they depended on each other for support.

Pulling out a chair across from Shannon, Jessie sank into it and waited until she heard floorboards creak upstairs. "I knew Gavin Bradley before he came to Four Oaks. He's Lisa's father."

Shannon whistled low through her teeth. "I saw the tension between you two at the picnic. Now I know what it was from."

"This is such a mess. Lisa likes him. He wants to tell her he's her father. And I'm not sure what's best for any of us."

"What do *you* feel?" Shannon asked. "About Gavin?"

"I don't know. I look at him and feel all quivery inside like a teenager. But that doesn't mean a thing. I felt that way before. I thought I loved him, and then he left and I found out I was pregnant. He says he broke up with me for *my* good. Can you believe that?"

"Can *you?*"

That's what Jessie liked about Shannon. She didn't pretend to have all the answers. "I don't know. But if he loved me and he left, he was wrong. Because now I can't believe he'll stay. If I give him my heart again..."

"Jessie, I'm not sure you've ever taken it back. You don't date. You work and live your life for Lisa. I think you gave it to Gavin all those years ago, and he still has it."

Did her heart still belong to Gavin? Now that he was here, maybe she *had* to explore her feelings for him or she'd never move on. What a sobering thought.

* * *

Jessie awakened with a start Wednesday morning, knowing it wasn't her alarm that had made her heart beat faster and her eyes fly open. Glancing to the side of her bed, she spotted her daughter. "Honey, what's wrong?"

"My ear hurts again, Mommy. Bad."

Jessie opened her arms to her daughter. "Come here."

Lisa crawled into bed beside her. Jessie switched off her alarm, which would ring in a few minutes, then she pressed her cheek against Lisa's forehead. "You don't feel warm."

"The room's crooked when I walk."

Jessie turned on the light and studied Lisa's face. Her color looked normal. But Jessie knew sometimes one prescription of antibiotics wasn't enough. Or maybe something else was wrong, something more serious.

"I guess I'll have to go see Dr. Bradley."

Jessie was already thinking about her morning appointments and how she could rearrange her schedule. "I'll call his office. You stay here in my bed and keep still. That way, you won't be dizzy. Do you feel sick or would you like some breakfast?"

"Toast and hot chocolate?"

She was thankful Lisa's stomach wasn't upset, but there was no point pushing it. "What about tea instead of hot chocolate?"

Lisa shrugged. "Okay."

"I'm going to make some phone calls, then I'll bring it up."

Gavin's receptionist fit Lisa in at ten o'clock. Jessie drove to the hospital, only concerned about her daughter, anxious to find out what was wrong. They didn't have to wait long.

The nurse showed Jessie and Lisa to an examining room, then took Lisa's temperature and made a notation on the chart. A few minutes later, Gavin entered the room with a frown. "What happened?"

His white long-sleeved shirt, charcoal slacks and striped tie made him seem even taller and more imposing than usual. When she stared into his worried gray eyes, she wondered if Shannon was right and he still held her heart. But this wasn't the time to think about her feelings for Gavin.

Jessie focused on his nose rather than letting his probing gaze learn too much. "She woke up this morning with an earache again and dizziness."

"You finished all of the antibiotic?"

Jessie nodded. "Yesterday."

Gavin cocked his head and studied his daughter. "Hop up there on the table for me, Lisa." He shifted a step stool with his foot so it stood in front of the table.

Gavin examined her ears, nose and throat. He asked her to do a few simple exercises like closing her eyes and touching her finger to her nose. Then he lifted her to the floor, had her stand up straight and hold out her hands with her eyes closed. When she smiled up at him, he patted her head.

"Lisa, how would you like to go play with the toys in the waiting room for a few minutes while I talk to your mom?"

"Cool! Are you going to give me more medicine?"

"We'll see. Are you still feeling dizzy?"

She walked to the door, then turned around and smiled at him. "I feel better."

"Good. C'mon. I'll tell Miss Robinson to let you play with some puppets. I'll bet you like the dog. His name is Alfred."

Lisa giggled and walked beside him down the hall.

A concerned Jessie watched her daughter leave the room. Why did Gavin want to talk to her alone? Maybe he found something more serious than an earache. If anything happened to Lisa...

Before she could consider his behavior further, Gavin returned. Closing the door, he lodged a hip against the examining table. "I think she's faking."

Jessie was shocked. "Why would she be faking?"

His expression was gentle as he offered, "Children fake illness for lots of reasons. Is there some reason she'd rather not be at school today?"

"Not that I know of. She does well at school. She likes her teacher and has plenty of friends. That isn't it. Maybe you're wrong. Maybe you missed something."

"I think we're both missing something, but it's not physical. Let's talk to her and find out."

"Gavin, nothing like this has ever happened before."

He covered her hand with his. "We'll get to the bottom of it."

Jessie's mind spun. Why would Lisa pretend to be sick? *Was* she afraid of something at school?

Gavin squeezed her fingers. "We *will* find out what's wrong," he reassured her again.

She knew he was speaking as a father, as well as a doctor. The thought was both comforting and unsettling.

Gavin left the examining room and returned a few moments later with Lisa. Jessie opened her arms to her. "Come here, honey. Dr. Bradley and I want to talk to you."

Looking worried, Lisa asked, "About my earache?"

Gavin pulled over a chair so he, too, was on Lisa's level. "*Do* you have an earache?"

The little girl glanced from him to Jessie. "It feels fine now."

Lifting Lisa's chin Jessie said, "We've talked about telling the truth and how important that is."

Lisa nodded and bit her lower lip.

"Did your ear hurt this morning?" Gavin asked.

This time Lisa shook her head, and her eyes began to grow shiny.

Jessie stroked her daughter's hair behind her ear. "Why did you say it did? Did you want to stay home from school?"

Again Lisa shook her head.

"Why, then?" Gavin's voice was gentle and deep, making Jessie realize just how much he really did care.

The eight-year-old ducked her head. "I wanted to see you again. Mom said I couldn't invite you to my recital and she wouldn't say when we'd see you.... *Are* you too busy?"

Guilt stabbed Jessie as she watched Gavin's expression.

His jaw tensed with anger, and he chose his words carefully, not taking his eyes from his daughter. "I'm busy. But not *too* busy to spend time with people I like."

"Do you like me and mom?" the child asked seriously.

"Yes, I do."

"See, Mom. He likes us and he's not too busy. Can we ask him to the recital?"

"Lisa, taking up Dr. Bradley's office time when you're *not* sick is wrong. And not telling me the truth is also wrong. Do you understand that?"

Her daughter nodded. "Are you going to punish me by not letting Dr. Bradley come?"

"Dr. Bradley might be working...."

"When is it?" he asked, his voice even.

"Sunday afternoon," Lisa piped up.

"I'm on call. If I don't have any emergencies, I can be there. But, Lisa, your mother has to do what she thinks is best for you."

"Mom?"

Jessie wanted to scream. How had her life gotten so complicated in such a short amount of time? "I think you need to know that what you did today was wrong."

"I know, Mom."

"So *I* know you really know, you can do without your skateboard for a week."

"Aw, Mom..."

Jessie raised her brows, and Lisa agreed, "Okay. But can Dr. Bradley come?"

"If he wants to."

"I can't think of many things I'd rather do."

His voice was laced with an undercurrent, and Jessie could imagine exactly what those other things were.

He stood and pushed back his chair. "I have to get to my other patients. I'll call you for the particulars."

Feeling as if she were fighting against a tidal wave, Jessie told him, "It's two o'clock at the middle-school auditorium. No tickets."

"Sounds good. And how would you two like to go to dinner afterward?"

"Oh, Mom, can we?"

Jessie felt Gavin was pushing and knew by his expression that he knew he was, as well. "My dad will be coming to the recital."

"He's invited," Gavin said with a challenge.

With the expression on her daughter's face, Jessie couldn't say no. "All right. I'll tell him."

Gavin opened the examining-room door, and they went into the hall. Lisa bounded ahead.

"I thought you were going to give me some breathing space," Jessie murmured to him.

"And I never thought you'd put words into my mouth. I'm never too busy to find time for Lisa. Understand?"

The anger was still there, and she supposed she deserved it. "I understand."

Gavin reached the receptionist's window before Jessie did. Leaning in, he told the woman behind the desk, "There's no charge for Lisa today."

Then he took the chart from a nearby examining-room door and said to Jessie, "I'll see you Sunday." Without waiting for her to respond, he opened the door and greeted his next patient.

She couldn't argue with Gavin's decision not to accept payment, nor his desire to take care of his daughter. Jessie curved her arm around Lisa's shoulders and guided her into the waiting room, wondering how she was going to tell her father Gavin would be joining them on Sunday. Even more worrisome was wondering what her father's reaction would be.

Knowing the confrontation with Owen Windsor had been long in coming, Gavin rode the elevator to the businessman's office. Since Windsor owned the building of condominium suites, he'd chosen the top floor for his business dealings—of course. Only the best, the most and the highest for Owen Windsor.

Gavin had decided the best offense would be a surprise offense. He hadn't made an appointment because he didn't want Windsor to be prepared.

When the elevator doors opened, Gavin stepped onto plush taupe carpeting. He followed the short corridor to double glass doors inscribed with Windsor Plastics, Incorporated. Opening the door, he stepped inside.

Walking up to the front secretary's desk, he said, loud enough for the two secretaries positioned behind her to hear, "I'd like to see Owen Windsor. I don't have an appointment. But if you tell him Gavin Bradley is here, I'm sure he'll make time.''

The secretary lifted the phone and relayed the message. After a brief conversation, she pointed down another short corridor. ''First door. Mr. Windsor will open it from inside.''

Gavin had to smile as he stood in front of the door, feeling as if he were waiting to get beamed onto a spaceship. But his smile faded as the door slid open and Owen Windsor scowled at him from behind a massive desk.

Gavin approached the desk, but Jessie's father didn't give him the courtesy of standing.

''What do you want, Bradley?''

''Hello, Mr. Windsor. It's good to see you again, too, after all these years. I thought we could start out on a different foot this time.''

Windsor stood then, but as a defensive measure, not as a courtesy. ''As far as I'm concerned, nothing has changed. Do you think I didn't do some checking when I learned you were coming here? You may be a doctor now, but all you own is a car. You've started paying back loans, but it will be a while until they're paid off.''

''You sure do have a hang-up about money, don't you?'' Gavin asked, curious why this man was still fighting his place in Jessie's life.

''That's where you're wrong. I have a hang-up about breeding. Jessica and I have a reputation to maintain in this community. Your background is abominable. A society columnist looking into your past would have a field day. Alcoholic father. Illiterate mother.''

Gavin didn't think about his background. He couldn't if he wanted to move forward. He'd never lied about his upbringing but he never shared it with anyone other than his closest friends, either. "And what about a society columnist looking into Jessie's past, revealing she had a child out of wedlock. Would you find that embarrassing, too?''

Windsor's face reddened. "Jessica made one mistake, and I've made sure she doesn't suffer for it.''

"You've paid people off, haven't you, so they wouldn't look at the situation too closely?''

"I do what I have to do.''

"Like the pep talk you gave me nine years ago.''

Windsor remained silent.

"Jessie doesn't know about that, does she?''

The man's expression rivaled the stone faces on Mt. Rushmore.

"Tell me, did you intercept the letter I sent her?''

"I think you'd better leave, Bradley.''

"And I think you'd better make up your mind to get along with me. This time I won't brook any interference from you. This time, I'll be fighting for my daughter, as well as for Jessie.''

Windsor leaned forward, his hands braced on the desk. "Are you so certain Lisa *is* your daughter? Jessica's a beautiful girl. As soon as she came home that summer, her old boyfriends were buzzing around her like bees. I convinced her that waiting for you would be a monumental mistake, and she took my advice and dated them.''

For a moment, just a moment, Gavin wondered if Windsor could be right. Jessie had been a virgin when they made love. But when Gavin didn't call her, could she have turned to someone else for comfort? Did she really know that Lisa *was* his child?

Then his good sense reigned. Jessie would never tell him Lisa was his daughter unless she knew for sure. Windsor was just trying to drive another wedge between them.

"Get used to me being around, Mr. Windsor. I lost Jessie once. I won't lose her again. And if you try to interfere, I will tell her everything you've done to 'protect' her."

"Get out, Bradley. Before I call security."

Gavin couldn't understand the man's obsession with breeding. He couldn't understand why Windsor couldn't accept him as he was and work with him for his daughter's and granddaughter's happiness. Maybe one day he would understand. But for now, he wouldn't let Jessie's father stand in his way.

"You're a stubborn man, Mr. Windsor. But I can be just as stubborn. You're still invited to dinner after Lisa's recital."

Jessie's father looked surprised for a moment. But then the surprise vanished. He stood in silence waiting for Gavin to leave.

When Gavin reached the corridor and the door silently closed behind him, he wondered what he'd have to do to earn Owen Windsor's approval. And suddenly he realized how Jessie must feel and how strong she'd been to live her life without it. He'd always admired Jessica Windsor. Now he admired her even more.

Chapter Five

The middle-school auditorium buzzed with the sound of family and friends prepared to see their children perform. The desire in Gavin to claim his child publicly was strong and demanding. But his relationship with Jessie was still too tenuous to push her further.

Gavin had never been a man to sit back and wait for opportunities to happen. Ever since childhood, he'd created his own opportunities, then worked to accomplish his goals. He would be a father to Lisa. Soon.

The auditorium provided more than enough seats. Most rows weren't filled. Gavin found Jessie in the center section next to her father. Two seats beside her sat vacant.

Excusing himself to the family on the end of the row, Gavin sat down beside Jessie.

She glanced at her father, then back at Gavin, a worried expression on her face. "Gavin, this is my father, Owen Windsor."

Gavin extended his hand to the man, giving him another opportunity to bury the hatchet. But Owen Windsor ignored the gesture.

Gavin wouldn't lie to Jessie. "We've already met."

Jessie's mouth rounded, and Gavin thought he detected a flicker of fear in Owen Windsor's eyes. "I visited your father's office the other day to discuss Lisa's welfare. And yours."

Jessie frowned. "Dad, why didn't you tell me?"

Her father shrugged. "There was no reason to tell you. Bradley and I disagree about what's best for you and my granddaughter. I'd just as soon he disappear."

"Dad!"

Gavin sat back in his seat and covered her hand. "It's all right. Your father and I came to an understanding." He leaned closer to Jessie, his lips almost brushing her ear. "Like you, he just needs some time."

Jessie turned, whether to agree or disagree, he didn't know. But her lips almost touched his. Her beautiful blue eyes, her pink mouth, her perfume wafting about his head like a sensual cloud, urged him to kiss her right then and there. Good sense told him to raise his head and remember where he was.

She cleared her throat and looked straight ahead. The lights in the auditorium dimmed, and Gavin kept his hand on hers. "Was Lisa nervous?"

Jessie shook her head. "Not a bit. She's been waiting for this day for weeks. One of her friends started crying yesterday afternoon at the dress rehearsal because she forgot her steps. Lisa hugged her and told her to just listen to the music and pretend she's alone in her room practicing."

Gavin said quietly, "That's one to remember." He'd missed so much . . . so many memories.

Jessie leaned closer until her shoulder grazed his. "You'll have today to remember."

The compassion in her voice told him she still cared even if she didn't realize it. He squeezed her fingers. "And many more, I hope."

She went still beside him. He might as well face it. He didn't know how *not* to push.

When the curtain rose, Jessie withdrew her hand and leaned forward. Gavin's touch was too much of a distraction. She wanted to concentrate on her daughter. *Their* daughter, she reminded herself. Even though Gavin had made himself clear about making time for Lisa, Jessie had expected an emergency to crop up. She'd expected him to be late or unavailable. . . .

It wasn't just Gavin. As a child, Jessie had known her father's work had always come first—before tucking her in at night, before her piano recital, before just about everything. She didn't want Lisa to experience the same disappointment she herself had experienced. With the nature of Gavin's profession, his work had to come first. There was nothing Jessie could do about that except try to explain it to Lisa.

Concentrating on the performance before her, she tried to block out the scent of Gavin's soap—the same one he'd used in college. He'd always smelled like man and soap, and she'd always found it exciting. He was so long waisted and broad shouldered that she felt little beside him. As he shifted his legs, she had to smile. Auditorium seats weren't designed for tall men.

When Lisa finally made her entrance, Jessie's throat tightened. She nudged Gavin's elbow, and in a husky voice, he said, "I see her. She looks beautiful, doesn't she?"

Jessie just nodded.

Time seemed to speed by, though Jessie wanted to hold on to every moment and slow it down. "I've got to get a video camera," she murmured as the flowers danced around the trees and ladybugs flittered in and out.

At the end of the ballet, no one clapped more enthusiastically than Gavin. "She was terrific!"

Owen Windsor stood, his slight smile fading as he glanced at Gavin, but said to Jessie, "You tell Lisa she did a fine job."

"You could tell her yourself," Jessie responded. "Even if you're not going to dinner, you could come with me backstage."

He frowned. "I don't want to get mixed up in all that. I'll see you two next Sunday for dinner, right?"

"I'll let you know if something comes up. Thanks for coming, Dad. I know it means a lot to Lisa."

Owen leaned closer to Jessie and said, "You watch your step. You don't want to make another mistake."

Automatically anger rose, and Jessie bit her tongue. Her father would never change. She knew he was already prejudiced against Gavin. What father wouldn't be when a man got his daughter pregnant, then left? That's the way her father would always see it. But Jessie had to hope time would change her father's opinion of Gavin, especially if Gavin was going to be an active parent in Lisa's life.

"As I've told you before, Dad, you're going to have to trust my judgment."

With a "Hmph" and a glare at Gavin, Owen left.

Jessie sighed and took a deep breath. When she turned, she saw Gavin watching her closely.

"How do you put up with that?"

"He's my father."

"You're fighting to be your own person and earn his love at the same time. Have you always done that?"

"Always. Dad is . . ."

"Hard," Gavin filled in with more conclusiveness than she'd expected. But then she didn't know exactly what Gavin and her father had said to each other the other day.

"He's stubborn," she offered instead. "He thinks he always knows best. But he cares about me, Gavin. I didn't always believe that, but over the years I've come to realize it."

"He has preconceived notions that make dealing with him difficult."

"Did the two of you argue?"

"We disagreed. He doesn't want me in your life. I told him I'm in it already."

The determination on Gavin's face excited Jessie and scared her. Could she let him into her life again? Could she take that risk?

He took her hands in his and looked deep into her eyes. "I went to see your father to reach some kind of an understanding with him. But I can see understanding isn't his strong suit."

"What do you want me to say, Gavin?"

"You don't have to say anything. I want you to make up your own mind about us even if your father tries to interfere."

"How can he interfere?"

Gavin's gray eyes darkened and the jut of his jaw sharpened. "I don't know if he can. But if you have questions or doubts about what I say or do, you come to me about it. Understand?"

She wasn't exactly sure what Gavin meant. He seemed to be accusing her father of something.... Maybe it was her imagination. "I don't confide in Dad. I never have. And I do make up my own mind. Nine years ago, you didn't give me the opportunity. You made the decision for me."

He caressed her cheek. "It's going to take a while for that anger and hurt to fade away. But if you give it a chance, if you give *us* a chance, it will."

When he touched her, she could almost believe it. When he touched her, anything seemed possible. The moment was too intense, too filled with an almost-promise. "I've got to get backstage."

"I'm coming with you."

She had to smile. "Not into the girls' dressing room you're not."

He gave her a crooked grin. "I'll wait outside."

Backstage, Jessie sent Lisa to change into street clothes. While she waited for her daughter, she found Shannon. "Gavin's here," Jessie told her friend. "So we won't need a ride home."

Shannon's green eyes were concerned. "When I looked over, your dad was glaring at him. Is everything all right?"

"As all right as it can be right now. I'd better help Lisa with her makeup before she streaks it all over her face."

Shannon nodded knowingly.

Not wanting to keep Gavin waiting, Jessie helped her daughter pack up. Lisa bubbled over with excitement about the performance, her makeup and Gavin and her grandfather sitting in the audience. "I saw Dr. Bradley watching me," she said as she waved goodbye to Marly and pushed open the dressing-room door. Seeing him leaning against the wall, she ran to him. "What did you think?"

He smiled a proud-father's smile. "I think you were the most talented ballerina performing."

She giggled. "I only made one mistake. But I don't think anybody noticed."

"I didn't see any mistakes." He grinned at Jessie. "Did you?"

"Not a one."

"Can I wear my costume at home?"

"Why?" Jessie asked as she transferred the hanger to her other hand.

"I don't know. But I want to wear it again."

"Maybe you and Marly can dress as twin ballerinas for Halloween," Jessie suggested.

Lisa turned up her nose. "Nah. But maybe we could dance for you and Dr. Bradley sometime. Just our parts."

"A private performance," Gavin added. "That sounds good. Maybe you can get your mom to sing or hum along."

"Hey, neat idea. Or better yet, Mom, you can be the tree."

"Actually I think Dr. Bradley looks more like a tree," Jessie teased.

He gave them a mock scowl. "You won't get me in tights."

Lisa giggled. "We'll just give you some leaves to hold."

As Gavin drove them to a family restaurant, the teasing and joking continued. Jessie couldn't remember smiling and laughing so much in years. Gavin had a great sense of humor. She'd forgotten that. Just as she'd forgotten the wonderful warm feeling inside her whenever his deep laughter vibrated through her.

She'd also forgotten how well he listened, not only to her, but to Lisa. It was as if his daughter's every word was important.

They were finishing the ice cream they'd ordered for dessert when Lisa asked, "So when can you come over and watch me and Marly dance?"

"What about Tuesday? I'm on call, but unless there's an emergency, I should be able to get away by seven-thirty. Is that too late?"

"That's my last day of school. I get to go to bed a half hour later in the summer. Right, Mom?"

Jessie laughed. "How can I forget? You've been reminding me for the past two weeks. Tuesday is fine with me." She understood Gavin's need to be part of his daughter's life. She just wasn't sure how he fit into hers.

"What do you do during the summer while your mom works?"

"I stay with Marly. It's great."

"Is she your best friend?"

Lisa nodded.

Jessie remembered Gavin's best friend from college. "Did you stay in touch with Nathan Maxwell?"

"Not as much as I would have liked. But he's living in Roanoke. I called him soon after I got to Four Oaks. We saw each other in January at a friend's wedding."

"Is he married?"

"Divorced about a year ago."

"That's a shame." When Gavin didn't respond, she could see he wasn't going to talk about his friend. Jessie had liked Nathan. Shy and inexperienced with men, she'd appreciated his attempts to draw her out, to get to know her because she was spending time with Gavin.

"Mom, are you and my dad divorced?" Lisa asked.

The question jolted Jessie. Her gaze met Gavin's. "No, honey. Your dad and I never married."

"Because he left before I was born."

Jessie's mouth went dry, hoping Gavin wouldn't use Lisa's question as an opening to tell her he was her father. "Yes."

Gavin's jaw tensed, and he closed his hand into a fist on the table. But he kept silent.

Fortunately Lisa let the subject pass as quickly as it had come up. But some of the laughter disappeared from the day.

Gavin was quiet as he drove Jessie and Lisa home. They were just about to enter the house when Lisa spotted Marly on her skateboard. "Can I go ask her about Tuesday night?"

"Go ahead."

Once inside the foyer, Jessie turned to Gavin. "I know you wanted to tell her you're her father."

"Damn right I did."

"Thank you for not telling her."

He raked his hand through his hair. "I'm trying to do what's best for her, too."

"And I appreciate it."

He cupped Jessie's chin in his hand. "I don't want your appreciation."

"Gavin..."

"I know. I should stop pushing. Tell me something, Jessie. When you came home after graduation, did you date?"

The look on Gavin's face was too serious for this to be simply a trip down memory lane. "No, I didn't. I was waiting for you to call."

"And when I didn't?"

"Gavin, what are you getting at?"

"Are you sure I'm Lisa's father?"

"Of course I'm sure. I've never—" She stopped.

He clasped her shoulders and ordered in a husky murmur, "Finish it."

She felt the words tie up her tongue. Calming herself, she took a few measured breaths and said the words to herself before she said them aloud. "I've never been with anyone else."

He slid his hand under her hair. "What are you waiting for?"

She shook her head, feeling breathless and flushed. "I don't know."

He lowered his head. Before his lips touched hers he whispered, "I think I do."

Years slipped away, moments passed in heartbeats, the present became more important than anything that had gone before. Jessie realized she had never wanted another man, had never dreamed of another man, had never expected to fall in love again. Because Gavin had hurt her so badly? Because she'd been afraid to take the risk again? Because no other man could make her feel as deeply as Gavin had? She didn't have the answers and she couldn't find them with Gavin holding her as if she were something precious, kissing her as if he'd never thought of kissing anyone else.

Gavin's tongue slipped between her lips, breaching her defenses, coaxing her to believe they could have a future, as well as a past. Now that he'd captured her mouth, he took his hand from her hair and passed it down her back, pressing her closer. Her hands gripped his arms as his hard planes met her softer curves and passion became more than a lost dream.

Gavin knew he shouldn't push Jessie, shouldn't rush her. But her admission that she'd never made love with another man had made him reckless. If he could penetrate her walls, remind her what their desire had meant, convince her to trust him, all the years of work and sacrifice and hardship would make sense.

He cupped her bottom, holding her tight against him, telling her in the most honest way he could how much he wanted her. For a few seconds, she arched into him, making his arousal painfully evident.

Then abruptly she broke off their kiss and pulled back, stepping away from him, swaying from the intensity of their coming together.

He caught her shoulders to steady her, to keep her from withdrawing completely. "Jessie, don't be afraid of it . . . of us."

"But I *am* afraid. This time it's not only my heart involved, but Lisa's, too."

He brushed tendrils of hair from her flushed cheek. "I think Lisa and I are doing just fine. It's you and I that I'm concerned about."

Jessie pulled away from him. "You're her father and I'm her mother. I'm not sure there is a 'you and I.'"

He held her chin in his hand and ran his thumb over the soft point of it. "All your doubts and fears won't douse the passion that's always been between us. They won't keep me away, either." Dropping his hand, he opened the door. "I'll see you Tuesday night. In the meantime, think about that kiss. And the next one."

Before she could argue with him, he stepped outside. He felt like whistling. Step by step, they'd find their way back to each other. Step by step.

Jessie's pulse rate increased as she tidied up after supper on Tuesday. It was always like that when she knew she'd be seeing Gavin. Just the thought of him...

She shut a cupboard door with a forceful bang. She'd been in control of her life for the past nine years, and his unexpected reappearance had stirred up insecurities she'd thought she'd put to rest. It had also stirred up feelings she'd never expected to experience again. She thought about his question, *What are you waiting for?* She'd had no interest in dating anyone. She'd had no interest in finding a father for her daughter. Why?

Had she unconsciously been waiting for Gavin to come back into her life?

That was ridiculous. Just because she'd loved him once...

Maybe her heart knew better than her mind. Maybe she should listen to it.

And maybe you'll get hurt again if you do.

Ah, the voice of caution. She knew it well.

Marly and Lisa giggled and chattered as they dressed in their recital clothes. As seven-thirty approached, they came down to the living room, set up the tape player and made sure everything was ready.

GAME CARD 1

Win $ TRIPLE LUCKY Lotto

Up To $1,000,000

Scratch off Gold Panel on tickets 1-7 until at least 5 (hearts) are revealed on one ticket. Doing so makes you eligible for a chance to win one of the following prizes: Grand Prize, $1,000,000.00; 1st Prize, $50,000.00; 2nd Prize, $10,000.00; 3rd Prize, $5,000.00; 4th Prize, $1,000.00; 5th Prize, $250.00; 6th Prize, $10.00.

GAME CARD 4

Win $ TRIPLE LUCKY Lotto

Up To $1,000,000

Scratch off Gold Panel on tickets 1-7 until at least 5 (hearts) are revealed on one ticket. Doing so makes you eligible for a chance to win one of the following prizes: Grand Prize, $1,000,000.00; 1st Prize, $50,000.00; 2nd Prize, $10,000.00; 3rd Prize, $5,000.00; 4th Prize, $1,000.00; 5th Prize, $250.00; 6th Prize, $10.00.

GAME CARD 7

Win $ TRIPLE LUCKY Lotto

Up To $1,000,000

Scratch off Gold Panel on tickets 1-7 until at least 5 (hearts) are revealed on one ticket. Doing so makes you eligible for a chance to win one of the following prizes: Grand Prize, $1,000,000.00; 1st Prize, $50,000.00; 2nd Prize, $10,000.00; 3rd Prize, $5,000.00; 4th Prize, $1,000.00; 5th Prize, $250.00; 6th Prize, $10.00.

Win$ **TRIPLE LUCKY** Lotto

Up To $1,000,000

Scratch off Gold Panel on tickets 1-7 until at least 5 (hearts) are revealed on one ticket. Doing so makes you eligible for a chance to win one of the following prizes: Grand Prize, $1,000,000.00; 1st Prize, $50,000.00; 2nd Prize, $10,000.00; 3rd Prize, $5,000.00; 4th Prize, $1,000.00; 5th Prize, $250.00; 6th Prize, $10.00.

Win$ **TRIPLE LUCKY** Lotto

Up To $1,000,000

Scratch off Gold Panel on tickets 1-7 until at least 5 (hearts) are revealed on one ticket. Doing so makes you eligible for a chance to win one of the following prizes: Grand Prize, $1,000,000.00; 1st Prize, $50,000.00; 2nd Prize, $10,000.00; 3rd Prize, $5,000.00; 4th Prize, $1,000.00; 5th Prize, $250.00; 6th Prize, $10.00.

Win$ **TRIPLE LUCKY** Lotto

For FREE BOOKS

Scratch off the Gold Panel. You will receive one FREE BOOK for each ★ that appears. See the back of this Game Card for details.

They decided on a last-minute practice as seven-thirty came and went. Jessie felt her anger building as the hands on the clock approached eight and there was no word from Gavin. To keep the girls occupied, she popped popcorn and poured glasses of iced tea. But by eight-thirty, their disappointment showed.

"He's not coming, is he?" Lisa asked.

"I don't know what to tell you, honey."

Marly offered, "Maybe he forgot."

"Can you call him, Mom?" Lisa's tone suddenly grew hopeful.

Jessie went to the kitchen phone and dialed Gavin's apartment number rather than his pager. After all, this wasn't an emergency. She let it ring ten times. "He's not there, sweetheart. You know he said he was on call."

Her daughter frowned. "He said he'd come."

"If he didn't have an emergency."

"But he didn't call."

"I know. But maybe he couldn't. Marly, why don't you call your mom and see if she'll let you stay overnight. Then you and Lisa can have a pajama party."

"And stay up late?"

"How's ten o'clock?"

Lisa and Marly exchanged glances, then nodded. Lisa looked a little happier as Marly called Shannon. Her best friend's smile said her mother had given her permission to stay. Then Marly held out the phone to Jessie. "She wants to talk to you."

Jessie took the receiver. "Go on up and get out of your costumes."

The girls bounded out of the kitchen as she put the phone to her ear.

"Are you sure it's okay?" Shannon asked.

"It's a consolation prize. Gavin didn't show up."

"Jessie..."

"With Marly here, hopefully Lisa will forget her disappointment."

"Will you?" her friend asked.

"I'm not thinking about me right now. I'll see you tomorrow morning about eight."

After Jessie hung up, she felt tears prick her eyes. She blinked them away. But it wasn't as easy to blink away the pain in her heart.

Lisa and Marly were painting each other's fingernails with Jessie's nail polish when the phone rang at nine-thirty. Jessie picked it up, took a deep breath and said, "Windsor residence."

"Jessie, it's Gavin."

She remained silent.

"I had an emergency. A woman delivered a baby who was in distress. I couldn't get away to call."

"You don't have to explain to me, Gavin. Lisa is the one who was disappointed."

He swore. "Jessie, don't take this as a personal insult."

"I'm not."

"Like hell you're not," he muttered. "Would you let me talk to Lisa, or is she already asleep?"

"She's still up. I'll get her." She held the phone out to her daughter. "It's Dr. Bradley."

Lisa scrambled up from the floor and took the receiver.

Jessie watched her daughter as she listened to Gavin. Suddenly the eight-year-old smiled and said to Jessie, "Dr. Bradley wants to know if we'll be going to the hospital party on Saturday."

The yearly fete drew almost everyone in Four Oaks. "We'll be going around suppertime," Jessie answered.

Lisa relayed the information to Gavin. A few moments later, she asked him, "Do you want to talk to Mom again? Okay, I'll tell her. I'll see you Saturday." After she hung up, she turned to Jessie. "He said he was sorry he couldn't come tonight. A baby needed him. He wants us to meet him at the puppet booth on Saturday."

"Do you want to?" Jessie asked.

"Sure. He said he won't be on call Saturday so he'll be there. He promised."

"Something else might come up...." Jessie cautioned.

"He promised, Mom. He'll be there."

Jessie could remember a time when she'd been as naive as her daughter. "You and Marly get ready for bed now. I'll come up and tuck you in in a few minutes."

"Can we leave on the nail polish?"

Jessie nodded.

A half hour later, with the girls in bed, Jessie went downstairs to make herself a cup of tea. She knew sleep would be slow coming tonight. When the doorbell rang, she thought about not answering it. But if it was Gavin, she suspected he wouldn't give up easily.

Taking a deep breath, she went to the living room and opened the door.

Chapter Six

Meeting Gavin's gaze, Jessie steeled herself against Gavin's presence. She had to stop her heart from racing and her temperature from soaring whenever she got within a foot of him.

"Don't shut me out, Jessie." His voice was low but carried the edge of authority. Gavin always projected authority. Right now it only fueled her anger.

"I'm not shutting you out. You're the one who didn't show up."

His gray eyes became as cold as slate. "Can I come in?"

Jessie stepped aside, and he paced to the sofa, looked at it but didn't sit. When he turned to face her, Jessie waited for his apology. He'd opened the top button of his shirt; his tie hung loose around his neck as if he'd tugged it down. His white shirt was wrinkled, and he'd rolled up the cuffs. Contrary to her decision to stop it from racing, her heartbeat speeded up.

"You have to understand something, Jessie. My commitment to Lisa has nothing to do with unlimited time and everything to do with the time I do spend with her."

"And how do broken promises and her disappointment fit in with that philosophy?"

"I'm a doctor, Jessie. I won't apologize for that or the time and care I give my patients. When someone else is on call, I can make a promise. Otherwise, I can't."

"And you think Lisa can understand that?"

"I hope so. I'm going to explain it to her again on Saturday. What I want to know is can *you* understand it?"

His gaze searched her face until she wasn't sure how to answer.

Gavin raked his hand through his hair. "This is exactly why I left nine years ago. I couldn't put you through early mornings, late nights, thirty-six-hour shifts."

Jessie was torn between understanding Gavin's lifework and the still-fresh hurt of him cutting her out of his life without even asking her what she wanted. "I understand your dedication."

"Maybe part of you does, but there's something else going on, too. What is it?"

"I'm worried about Lisa—"

He shook his head. "How much was your dad around when you were a child?"

"I...he..." She turned away. "It doesn't matter."

He caught her arm. "I think it does. When were your parents divorced?"

"I was too young to remember."

"But your dad got custody?"

The ache tightened around Jessie's heart. "My mother fell in love with someone else and left."

"And your dad?"

"What do you want to know, Gavin? I don't know what you're looking for."

"Did your dad know how to take care of a little girl? Or did he let someone else do it?"

"I had a nanny."

"And your dad wasn't around much at all, was he?" Gavin guessed.

"My dad had a business to run. He..." Jessie stopped before she stuttered, before the sense of loneliness and feeling unloved by both of her parents became more than a memory.

Gavin laid his palm against her cheek. "I'm not like your father, Jessie."

She pulled back and spoke slowly, thinking about each sentence before she let it out. "You don't know my father. You don't know the pain he went through when my mother left. I've seen pictures of her. Looking at me reminded him of her. That's probably why he worked so hard, why he couldn't be around me."

"But you've forgiven him," Gavin decided with an edge to his voice.

She couldn't blame her father for a past neither he nor she could change. "Yes."

"Then why can't you forgive me?"

Tears welled up in her eyes. "It's not the same, Gavin."

He studied her for what seemed like forever. "No, I guess it's not," he said quietly. "It's getting late. I'd better go."

Her thoughts were as confused as her heart, but she followed him to the door.

Gavin stood close enough to kiss her. But he didn't. He gently brushed a tendril of hair from her brow. "I will be there on Saturday, Jessie. I'll see you around five at the puppet booth. Until then, think about letting some of your anger at me out. It might help you forgive."

One moment he was there, and the next he wasn't. Jessie closed and locked the door in more turmoil than she'd felt since she'd discovered she was pregnant.

Twenty minutes after he left Jessie's town house, Gavin lifted his foot from the accelerator as he entered the outskirts of Roanoke. Following the directions Nathan had given him a few days before with the invitation to drop in anytime, Gavin easily found the apartment complex where his friend lived. With his cellular phone in his pocket in case his service needed to reach him, Gavin climbed the outside stairway to Nathan's second-floor apartment. Then he rang the bell and waited.

Nathan Maxwell opened the door, and a wide grin spread across his face. "What are you doing here this time of night? Don't doctors get up with the sun?"

Gavin looked over his old friend. He'd kept his football-player physique in top condition. He could have played pro ball but he'd chosen marriage with the hopes of having a family instead. The problem was the family never materialized, and his marriage had broken up because of it.

"I get up with the sun but tonight I needed..." He shrugged. "Let's just say I was too restless to sleep."

Nathan motioned him inside. "It's good to see you no matter what the reason."

Nathan's living room was sparse—a black vinyl couch and chair, table, floor light and television left plenty of room for the rowing machine. "I hate to say it, pal, but this looks like a bachelor pad."

Nathan arched a dark brow. "I am a bachelor...now."

Gavin sank into the armchair. "Any chance you and Elaine will get back together?"

"Not in this lifetime," Nathan said sadly. "Not being able to have children..." He shook his head. "The damnedest part of it is the doctors said there's no tangible reason why we couldn't, which left both of us wondering who's at fault."

"What about adoption?"

"Elaine didn't want to go through the years of waiting or take a risk on a private adoption. The truth be told, I think she just wanted to try again with someone else," he added bitterly. "I heard last week she's engaged."

"I don't know what to say."

"There's nothing *to* say. It's over."

"You'll meet someone."

Nathan sat on the arm of the sofa. "Maybe a family's not in the cards for me. I've never had one, maybe I never will." He shrugged. "The store keeps me busy. Need any gear? Don't doctors play golf?"

Nathan's sports store carried everything from weights to skis. "I never had time to do anything but jog. And now..."

"Now you and Jessica Windsor are finding common interests again?" Nathan asked with a sly smile, his green gaze curious.

"Jessie and I have a daughter. I found out soon after I came to Four Oaks."

Nathan was silent for a moment. "Do you know how lucky you are?"

"Yes, I do. But Jessie's having problems forgiving me for leaving."

"You didn't know."

"It doesn't matter. I left her. I don't think she'll ever forget that."

"Give her some time."

"I hope that's going to do it. But I don't know."

Nathan grimaced. "I always thought as I got older, I'd have more answers. I don't."

Gavin thought back to college, when he, Nathan and two other fraternity brothers, Cade and Jeff, had talked about where they'd be ten years after graduation. "Have you heard from Cade lately?"

"About a month ago. He and Randi are still act-ing like lovebirds. And Jeff and Katie should be hav-ing their baby any day now."

Randi and Cade had met at Jeff and Katie's wed-ding last August. Gavin was glad Cade and Jeff had found women to share their dreams.

Nathan stood. "I'll get us something to drink, then you can tell me about this daughter of yours."

Mothers, fathers but mostly children sat on the grass surrounding the puppet booth on Saturday. At first Jessie looked for Gavin milling around the area. But then Lisa, who'd already found a spot on the grass, tugged on Jessie's skirt.

"Mom, that's Dr. Bradley and Alfred."

Jessie switched her attention to the booth and rec-ognized the puppet from the pediatrician's waiting room, as well as Gavin's voice. The children all watched with rapt attention as Alfred told knock-knock jokes. They giggled and hooted and finally clapped as Alfred wound up his routine and waved goodbye.

As the crowd dispersed, Gavin emerged from the booth, his red T-shirt and jeans making him look like any other patron of the hospital fete. Before she could move closer to him, a woman stepped up to Gavin at the booth. Patti Rogers. She'd tied her blond hair back in a ponytail with a scarf. Her short white shorts showed off long, curvy legs. Just how often did the woman run into Gavin? At the hospital. In his back-yard.

Gavin talked with her for a few moments, then smiled and nodded toward Jessie. Patti's smile dimmed a bit. But when he walked toward Jessie and Lisa, she trailed along. Suddenly Jessie wished she'd worn something more fashionable than her white peasant blouse, flowered skirt and sandals.

Lisa jumped up. "Dr. Bradley. Can I hold Alfred?"

Gavin smiled and handed her the puppet. "He's all yours."

Patti nodded to Jessie and said, "I just thought I'd stop and say hello. Gavin told me you're having supper together. I didn't know you two knew each other."

It was obvious Patti was fishing for information, or more accurately, what Gavin's interest was in Jessie.

Gavin replied for her. "Jessie and I went to the same college."

"Oh, so you're old friends?" Patti pressed.

Gavin's smokey gaze as he glanced at Jessie made her breathing more rapid. "We're getting reacquainted," he explained without really explaining at all.

"I see. Well, maybe you and I can have dinner another time. Jessie, it was good to see you again. Enjoy your evening."

Patti Rogers's words were polite, but Jessie felt her tone held a challenge. As the woman walked away, Jessie asked, "Did she invite you to have dinner with her?"

"Actually I think it was a gyro at the Greek concession stand." His eyes twinkled, and Jessie felt like poking him in his well-chiseled jaw.

"Is that what you want to have for supper?" she asked.

He took Jessie's hand and folded it into the crook of his arm. "I'm open to suggestions."

"I want a hot dog and french fries," Lisa volunteered. "And ice cream for dessert."

"That sounds good to me," Gavin agreed. "Then we can explore the rest of the festival. I'm volunteering at one of the booths from seven-thirty to eight."

"Which one?" Jessie wasn't surprised he'd donate his time, but she wondered what type of booth he'd volunteer for.

He started walking, keeping Jessie's hand tucked in his arm. "It's a surprise. You'll have to wait and see."

The three of them walked along the canopy-covered stands, Gavin never far from Jessie's side. Their arms would brush, their eyes would meet, his fingers would touch hers, and the world would tilt. Could simple chemical attraction do that? Or maybe it *was* all the buried feelings she didn't know how to express.

She watched Gavin with Lisa as they entered the petting zoo. Her daughter giggled as a deer tried to chew the edge of her T-shirt. Lisa gazed up at Gavin with trust as he settled her on a Shetland for a pony ride.

At seven-fifteen, Gavin guided them away from the picnic table where they'd eaten toward the games of chance. They stopped at the dunking booth. Jessie recognized the teenager sitting on the bench. He was the son of a board member.

She looked up at Gavin with surprise. "You've got to be kidding."

He affectionately tapped her on the nose. "Nope. I'll be right back. Get your throwing arm warmed up."

A few minutes later, Gavin returned, and Jessie's breath caught. He was wearing navy swim trunks that left nothing to her imagination. He was so tall and hard and broad shouldered. All that bare skin, his hair-covered chest...

"Can I throw some balls?" Lisa asked.

Gavin pointed to the large red bucket. "They're three for fifty cents. You pay that lady selling tickets for the rides."

"Mom, please?"

"I'm going to get positioned," Gavin said. "Jessie, make sure you buy some ammunition yourself." He winked. "Don't let Lisa have all the fun."

Jessie gave Lisa money to purchase two tickets. Her daughter did, then stood ready, waiting for Gavin to seat himself in the middle of the bench. Grinning at her, he yelled, "C'mon. Give it your best shot."

Lisa wound up, took aim and missed the bull's-eye. Three times. Frustrated, she looked up at Jessie with a frown. "*You* try it."

But Jessie felt awkward trying to dunk Gavin. It didn't seem...right.

"C'mon, Jessie," he called to her. "You want to do it. You know you do."

A few people had stopped to watch. They coaxed her with "It's all good fun."

"Let her rip."

"You'll be doing him a favor cooling him off."

Gavin grinned and cupped his hands over his mouth. "Let's go, Jessie. Cool me off."

She picked up the first ball, aimed at the red circle within the white and threw hard. The ball slapped wood, the bench tilted and Gavin slid into the water. Standing, he swiped the rivulets out of his eyes. After the man in charge of the dunking booth reattached the bench, Gavin climbed up and looked Jessie straight in the eye saying, "Again, Jessie. C'mon. Use that second ball."

She aimed and shot. The bench slid sideways, and Gavin splashed into the water again. When he came up this time, he swiped his hair from his forehead and challenged, "You've got one more, Jessie. Put all that you've got behind it."

The onlookers cheered Jessie on as Gavin climbed onto the bench a third time. His serious gray eyes dared her to think about the past, how she felt about him leaving her, the hurt, the disappointment, the anger. She'd never learned how to let those feelings out. And now she thought about how much she'd once loved Gavin and how she'd sworn to herself never to open her heart to anyone like that again.

She looked at the ball, at Gavin, at the target. Readying herself, she drew back, brought one knee up and threw the ball harder than she'd ever thrown before. It made a resounding crack as it hit the red circle. The spring on the bench unlatched, and Gavin fell into the water for the third time.

"Three for three. You oughta try out for the Braves, lady," a man called from behind her.

"Mom, you're good!" Lisa said in awe.

Jessie thought she'd feel some relief after the third successful throw. She'd thought the feelings would sink back below the surface. But she found the adrenaline was still coursing through her body, all the emotion still vibrating even as she drew away from the pitching box so the next person could take his turn. She didn't look at Gavin; she couldn't.

She murmured to her daughter, "Let's go get something to drink."

While they stood at the lemonade stand, Marly and Shannon came up beside them. Marly urged Lisa, "Let's go try the ponies and the rides. Mom, can we?"

Shannon looked at Jessie. "It's up to you. I'll take them if you'd like."

Realizing she could use a few minutes to herself, Jessie dug in her pocketbook for a five-dollar bill. "Go ahead. I'll meet you at the bandstand. Okay?"

Shannon checked her watch. "Let's say nine o'clock. There are lines at all the rides."

Jessie nodded.

"Are you okay?" Shannon asked in a low whisper.

"I'm fine. Go on," Jessie urged. "I'll talk to you later."

With a last, concerned look, Shannon let the girls lead her away.

Jessie bought a lemonade and wandered from booth to booth, looking but not seeing. The lights on the stalls went on, giving the area a carnival atmosphere. Suddenly Gavin stood in front of her dressed in his jeans and T-shirt, his hair wet. Jessie looked at him and felt tears prick in her eyes.

He curved his arm around her shoulders. "Where's Lisa?"

"With Shannon and Marly."

Guiding Jessie behind one of the booths, he turned her toward him. "So...do you want to dunk me a few more times?"

"Gavin..."

"It's all right, Jessie. You've got to feel it to get rid of it."

"You don't understand. All my life, I've fought against being angry—at my mother, at my father..."

"At me."

She gazed up at him and admitted it. "Yes."

He caressed her cheek, accepting the anger, accepting her. "I think you and I need to spend time alone together. This is my weekend off. Let's take advantage of it. A friend of mine has a cabin near Natural Bridge. We could drive there tomorrow and spend the day."

Alone with Gavin. She hadn't really spent any time alone with him since he'd come to town. In fact, she'd avoided it. Because she was afraid of what might happen? It was time they both found out if there was anything between them to build on except sparks and kisses and a few short months of...whatever it had been.

"I'll have to cancel with my father again."

Gavin's steady gray eyes searched her face. "Is that a problem?"

"He might make it one. But Lisa and I can have dinner with him some night this week. Maybe that will pacify him."

"What about Lisa?"

"I'll talk to Shannon and see if she'll be home. Lisa's probably going to feel left out, though. I think she considers you 'her' friend."

Gavin's voice was deep and husky. "I need time to become 'your' friend. We can plan something special with Lisa, maybe for the Fourth of July."

She could put up obstacles between them or she could try to start eliminating them. "All right. I'll go with you tomorrow. Do you want me to pack a lunch?"

His crooked grin and the silver lights of desire in his eyes heated Jessie as he said, "We can stop at the store before we leave and get supplies. The cabin has a kitchen."

"But isn't this short notice? What if your friend is using it himself?"

"His wife is pregnant and due any day. That's the last place Jeff would take her. He wants to be five minutes from the hospital. Where are you meeting Shannon?"

"At the bandstand."

"I'll go to the car and call him, then meet you over there." Gavin kissed her lightly on the lips and headed for the parking lot.

Once Gavin made a decision, nothing stood in his way. *Not even you?* a suspicious voice asked. Jessie walked toward the bandstand, hoping she wasn't making a mistake, hoping this time she was wise enough to know when to give her heart and when to keep it safe.

Gavin drove up a narrow, winding road into the thick blue-green foliage of the mountains. Jessie had been quiet during the drive, and he wondered what she was thinking...and feeling. She'd always been so warm and friendly with everyone, he'd never realized she was much harder on herself. Or maybe that had happened in the nine years he'd been gone.

"Have you been here before?" she asked above the soft strains of the radio.

"No, but Jeff talked about the place when we got together for Cade's wedding. He said he and Katie needed a retreat from the world. But he's CEO of a computer-software company and she's a lawyer, so they don't get here as often as they'd like."

"Is this the same Jeff you talked about in college?"

Gavin nodded. "He and Cade were two years ahead of me and Nathan, but we lived on the same floor of the fraternity house and became good friends. The four of us have managed to stay in touch over the years."

The road suddenly forked, and Gavin veered toward the left. After about a mile, he drove off the asphalt onto a gravel lane. A few minutes later, he parked in front of an A-frame and whistled. "Some cabin. I should have known Jeff isn't the rustic type."

Gavin was out of the car and around at Jessie's door before she could comment. He offered her his hand. With a smile, she took it and climbed out. That smile. It had always made him want to give her the world.

Following Jeff's directions, Gavin went around the corner of the A-frame, found a large black rock lodged behind the spouting and scooped it from the ground. The top half of the rock twisted off, and he found the key inside.

"Clever," Jessie murmured.

They climbed the steps to the deck. Gavin turned the dead bolt to the French doors and stepped inside.

The first floor was spacious—a living room with a fireplace along one wall, a kitchen under the loft, a bathroom and utility room off of that. Pale gray carpeting and spruce-green-and-wine upholstered furniture created a soothing, relaxed home away from home. Gavin's gaze rose to the loft...the bedroom. When he glanced at Jessie, she was gazing at the loft, too.

He put his hand on her shoulder.

Startled, she jumped, then evaded his eyes. "We'd better unload the car. The milk might spoil...."

He lifted her chin. "We only drove an hour, and there's ice in the bag."

"Still..."

"Relax, Jessie. We're going to hike and fish and have a good time. Jeff said there are fishing rods in the closet in the kitchen. See what's there while I unload the car."

While Gavin returned to the car, Jessie opened the closet in the kitchen, finding canned goods and . . . fishing rods. *Relax,* Gavin had said. She took a deep breath. How could she relax when every time his gaze fell on her, he looked as if he wanted to kiss her? Or maybe she was just projecting her own thoughts. Except the vibrations that hummed back and forth between them weren't simply in her imagination.

A few minutes later, Gavin set the grocery bags on the counter, then stowed the perishables in the refrigerator. "Hiking or fishing first. Your call."

"Let's hike." Maybe she could walk off some of her nervous energy.

Not only had Gavin gotten directions from Jeff to the cabin, but he must have asked about the trails, as well. He forged ahead, away from the stream running along the back of the property. Did the man *always* know where he wanted to go?

Gavin set a pace Jessie could easily follow. He helped her up the steeper inclines, waited as she made her way over roots and fallen trees and offered her water from a bottle attached to his belt. They hiked for a good hour, talking about nothing important as they walked side by side, hiking in silence when the terrain grew rougher. When their stomachs growled for lunch, they started back. Inadvertently Jessie found herself relaxing.

At the cabin, they made sandwiches and took them to the redwood table on the deck. Jessie popped the lid on her can of soda and munched on a potato chip. The soft breeze ruffled her hair, and she almost felt . . . content.

Until Gavin said, "Tell me about your pregnancy."

During the morning, they'd talked about the area, the cabin, the wildlife and the weather. But when she raised her gaze to Gavin's, she knew that was about to change. "What do you want to know?"

"Everything." He shrugged and smiled. "Start with your cravings."

She smiled back. "Vanilla ice cream with strawberries. That was tough in November and December, because I wanted *fresh* strawberries."

He laughed. "Anything else?"

"Roasted peanuts. I couldn't get enough. But then, after I'd eat them I'd get such indigestion. . . ."

He let silence settle between them and he waited for more.

"I gained twenty-five pounds, and by the end of my pregnancy, I couldn't see my feet," she confessed.

"Did you take Lamaze classes?"

She took another swig of soda. "No. But I read everything I could get my hands on because I wanted to deliver naturally."

"Why didn't you take classes?" His gray eyes were probing.

She set the can on the table. "I was at college until Christmas break."

"Lisa wasn't born until the end of January."

Gavin had always been good at details. She realized there was no point in hedging. "I didn't have a coach."

A pained look crossed his face. "Was your dad with you during labor?"

"No, and I never expected him to be. But he was there. Waiting. The nurses were a big help. I did okay."

"She was a big baby," Gavin said, his voice low.

"How do you . . . ? Oh, as her doctor, you have access to her records."

"Eight pounds four ounces, and twenty-one inches long."

The fact that Gavin had checked touched Jessie. "She had a mop of black hair and the biggest eyes you've ever seen."

"Do you have many pictures of her first years?"

"Albums full. I'll pull them out of the closet, and you can take them along and look at them. I have a baby book, too. With all the firsts."

Gavin suddenly went very still, and the nerve in his jaw worked. Jessie took a deep breath, not knowing what question to expect next.

When it came, it almost stopped her heart.

"Did you hate me when she was born?"

Chapter Seven

Jessie didn't give Gavin a quick answer. Too many emotions piled up on one another. But as she simply felt for a moment, she knew the words *hate* and *Gavin* could never go together in the same sentence.

"No, I didn't hate you. I couldn't because I loved Lisa even before she was born. I wondered where you were...I wondered if you'd care. I would remember the night she was conceived and then I'd...hurt. But I knew I couldn't think about that or you because I had to concentrate on Lisa and our life."

"And you never expected me to contact you again?"

"You gave me no reason to expect anything. Nine years is a long time."

The line of Gavin's mouth tightened. "Yes, it is."

When the silence between them became so awkward she couldn't finish her sandwich, she asked a question she'd wondered about. "Why did you become a doctor?"

Gavin put down his sandwich and straightened his shoulders. "It's a solid profession."

"I know many doctors, Gavin. Some go into it for the life-style and prestige. Some because of their intelligence, their family pushing them, a larger sense of responsibility. What's your reason?"

"I care about children getting medical attention." His voice was remote, and Jessie felt as if a giant wall had just gone up between them.

"I know both your parents are dead. But was it their wish for you?"

"No."

That one word was supposed to effectively close the topic. But Jessie wouldn't let it. "You know everything about me, Gavin. I really don't know that much about you."

Gavin finished his sandwich and stood. "You know I graduated from college, I worked the past nine years to become a physician and I have good friends who can give you a written reference if I need it. Most of all, I care about you and Lisa. The rest doesn't matter."

"It matters to me."

"Well, it shouldn't. Let's go fishing."

"Gavin . . ."

"Drop it, Jessie. I don't want to talk about growing up or my parents. It has nothing to do with my life now." He motioned to her plate. "Are you finished?"

No. Not by a long shot. Something drove Gavin, something that made him the man he was today—purposeful, determined, dedicated. "You want me to open up to you, but you won't answer a few questions. Do you think that's fair?"

His gray eyes didn't waver from hers. "No. But that's the way it is."

The hard line he'd drawn hurt. Gavin wasn't a closed man, at least not the Gavin she thought she knew. Maybe she didn't know him at all.

The tension between them didn't diminish as Jessie opened a can of corn to use for bait, and Gavin carried the fishing rods and tackle box to the bank of the stream. As they sat on the edge, Jessie carefully speared kernels of corn with her hook.

Gavin said, "We could dig for live bait."

Jessie shrugged. "This is fine. If we don't catch anything, we can change our tactics."

As Gavin cast his line, Jessie watched the play of muscles under his T-shirt, the strength of his arm. Why was he so reluctant to talk about his past? Unless... Her mind started running wild. Maybe he'd gotten into trouble as a teenager. Maybe he'd been arrested or... She stopped the thoughts. That scenario didn't fit a pre-med student on scholarship.

Glancing at Gavin's profile, the strong, sometimes stubborn line of his jaw, she realized maybe she wasn't the only one who had a problem with trust.

The ripple of the stream, the call of birds, the leaves rustling gently with the warm breeze, should have lulled their cares away. But the peace and the gifts of a summer day intensified the strain between them. Jessie was too aware of the lock of black hair falling over Gavin's forehead, his male body—hot and powerful beside her, his scent—a mixture of soap and male, urging her to breathe deeper, move closer, touch him for no reason except she wanted to feel his skin against hers.

She stopped the merry-go-round of thoughts and the dizziness that went along with the desire. "I'm going to cast farther in." Standing, she moved away a few feet, then stepped onto one of the large rocks. To reach a deeper area of the stream, she gingerly hopped to another and then another.

Gavin slid a look at her. "Be careful, Jessie."

"I'm fine. I'm not catching anything in the shallow water. I'm just going to—" When she tried to hop to the next rock, the smooth, shiny surface was much more slippery than she expected. The sole of her sneaker slid sideways, and she fell on her backside into the gravel streambed. Feeling like an idiot, she held the fishing rod out of the water.

Gavin tossed his rod aside. Before she could even think about standing, he scooped her out of the water into his arms and carried her to the bank. "You weren't careful."

His voice rumbled in his chest, and somehow she'd dropped the fishing rod and her arms had encircled his neck. "I tried to be."

His gray eyes grew smoky as his heartbeat thudded against her shoulder. She could feel the quickening pace of her own heart. The lines along his mouth deepened slightly. She thought about touching his jaw, the line of his beard shadow . . .

Gavin set her on her feet. "You're all wet. Let's find some dry clothes."

Steadying herself, she glanced at his shirtfront. "You're not much better."

He slanted her a smile. "But my jeans are dry."

Jessie's clung to the backs of her knees. "I didn't bring along another pair."

He plucked her rod from where it had landed on the rocks, then fetched his and the tackle box. "We'll find something at the cabin."

Jessie's sneakers squished as she walked. She flipped them off on the deck along with her socks.

Gavin headed for the stairs, obviously expecting her to follow. "You and Katie are about the same size. If she—"

Jessie stayed at the foot of the steps. "I don't want to go through her things. If you could just find me a blanket or something, I can toss these in the dryer."

Gavin glanced at the bedroom upstairs and Jessie firmly planted on the first floor. "I'm sure Katie wouldn't mind."

Jessie shook her head. "I don't want to disturb her things."

When Gavin seemed to be waiting for more of an explanation, she added, "When I was growing up, our housekeeper would put things away in my drawers, rifle through them if she saw something she thought was out of place and put it where she thought it should be. It always felt like an invasion of privacy."

Gavin cocked his head. "It was. Go to the bathroom and get rid of those wet clothes. I'll find something."

Jessie found the bathroom and stripped off her clothes. Everything was soaked, including the back of her bra. Taking a fluffy green bath towel from the rack, she dried off, then wrapped it around her.

Gavin rapped on the door.

She opened it a crack, then a few inches. But when Gavin's gaze slipped from her shoulders to her bare feet, the door might as well have been wide open. The leap of her heart, the heat in his eyes, made her close her hand securely over the place where she'd tucked the end of the towel.

He held out a short white terry robe. "Katie's a practical lady. It was hanging on the back of the bedroom door."

Jessie took it from him. Their fingers touched, and she felt as if she'd been struck by lightning. She grabbed the robe tightly as the shock vibrated through her body.

She saw Gavin's jaw tense, his forehead crease, then he nodded to the pile of clothes on the floor. "Give me those and I'll throw them in the dryer."

Eager to close the door again, Jessie hung the robe on the towel rack and scooped the clothes from the floor. But as she straightened, her gaze collided with Gavin's. His dipped to the crevice at her breasts. Tingling with the awareness of what he wanted and what she was fighting against, she hauled in a deep breath, pushed the clothes into his arms and closed the door.

Jessie untucked the towel and slipped into the robe, belting it tight around the waist. It smelled as if it had just come from the dryer. She wished it had a few buttons and covered her knees, but it was better than the towel. As she opened the door, she heard the hum of the dryer.

When she went to the living room, Gavin was seated on the couch, bare-chested, a checkerboard and checkers on the coffee table in front of him. He'd opened the French doors and the windows. The beautiful summer day swept inside. The scent of pines wafted through the room.

Crossing to the sofa, Jessie sat a few inches from Gavin, trying to keep her eyes from lingering on the curly black hair on his chest, on the bronze nipples, on the line of hair leading to his belt buckle. Everything about him shouted *Danger—potent male*. Even his jean-covered thighs, spread wide as he set up the checkerboard, made her swallow hard.

Attempting to balance her equilibrium, which seemed totally out of whack since her fall, she remarked, "I guess you know Lisa thinks I'm the hottest checkers player in Four Oaks."

"Is that a challenge?" His grin was crooked, boyish and altogether endearing.

"That depends whether this is a friendly game or a competitive one."

His knee brushed hers as he turned toward her, his gray eyes settling on her lips and his voice deepening. "Definitely friendly."

The air in the room suddenly seemed nonexistent. Her mouth went dry. She could hardly breathe, let alone speak.

"Jessie..."

The raspy desire in his voice drew her toward him. He took her face between his hands and lowered his lips to hers.

Every time Gavin kissed her, she was surprised by the burst of passion, the want and need that intensified with each breath, each taste, each touch. When she braced her hands on his chest, sliding her fingers through the hair, he groaned and broke the seam of her lips with his tongue.

The heat radiating between them was intoxicating, magnetic, undeniable. His alone made her tremble. Hers combined with his made her shake. When his tongue swept her mouth, she held on to his shoulders, not sure the earth would ever stand still again. There had been so much distance between them. And she wanted it all gone. She wanted Gavin.

The kiss wasn't enough no matter how many times their tongues met or explored or danced against each other. Her hands roamed over Gavin's shoulders, his arms, remembering, rediscovering. He never broke their kiss as he laid her back on the sofa, coming down on top of her. His weight was exciting, and his jeans against her bare legs were arousing. His hips settled on hers, and every womanly desire inside her cried for fulfillment.

The belt on her robe gave way as Gavin trailed his hand up her thigh, and she gasped from the intimacy of his touch. He kissed her cheek, her neck, the pulse at her throat. When he nudged the robe apart with his chin and put his lips to the V between her breasts, she raked her nails down his back.

His response was to take her nipple between his lips and lave it with his tongue. Her womb contracted, and her breath hitched. They'd only been like this with each other once before—naked and free and giving to each other. She wanted to give. She wanted to give everything. . . .

An internal alarm went off so loud, her head echoed with it. Give everything? Again? When she still had doubts and anger and so many fears? No!

She didn't realize she'd said it aloud until Gavin raised himself on his elbows, his face flushed, his eyes glazed with desire. "What's wrong?"

The question held frustration and surprise. But it didn't matter. "I can't do this. *We* can't do this."

He closed his eyes for a moment, then shoved himself up. He ran his hand over his face, then looked at her. "Cover up, Jessie, before I decide I'm not a civilized man."

He looked a lot less than civilized with his hair disheveled, his gray eyes blazing with silver sparks aimed right at her, his broad shoulders glistening with the sheen of passion they'd shared. Hastily she pulled the robe together and sat up, a good foot away from him.

"I'm sorry. I didn't mean to lead you on or—"

"You don't have anything to be sorry for. Honest to God, Jessie, I didn't bring you here for that."

"Maybe our clothes are dry."

Shaking his head, he said, "Your jeans were pretty wet." He stood and dragged the upholstered chair toward the coffee table. "I think it's a good idea if you and I sit on opposite sides of the checkerboard." Then he opened the box of checkers and dumped them onto the board. "Red or black?"

"Red."

He started placing them on the board. "I think when the clothes are dry, we should move on to Natural Bridge . . . see the rock formations . . . explore the caverns . . . have dinner."

She nodded. The cabin was too conducive to intimacy. The longing was there but not the trust. And without trust, making love was out of the question.

Gavin's gaze met hers, and she knew he knew it, too.

The next two and a half weeks didn't settle Jessie's turmoil or give her peace of mind. Gavin had called to tell her Katie and Jeff were now the proud parents of a baby girl. He'd visited her and Lisa after office hours, learned how to skateboard from Lisa, taken Jessie to dinner and afterward given her a kiss on the lips that was much too chaste—long enough to make her heart race but short enough to keep fiery passion from rising. Whenever he looked at her, his gaze was somewhat guarded, hiding his thoughts. It was as if he was waiting for some sign from her that she was ready for the next step. But she wasn't exactly sure what that was.

When Gavin arrived on the Fourth of July to join in the celebration with Shannon, Ted and Marly, he wasn't smiling and looked worried. As Jessie opened the door, she asked, "What's wrong?"

"I have a patient in intensive care. A four-year-old with pneumonia."

She read the weariness on his brow. "You just came from there?"

He nodded.

"Is there anything more you can do?"

"No. And that's what's so frustrating. I'm hoping he'll respond in the next couple of hours. So I just wanted to warn you I could get paged at any time."

Gavin getting paged was nothing new. In fact, she was getting used to it. Right now she was more concerned about the tension riding his brow than having their evening interrupted. She pointed to the hassock in front of the chair. "Sit."

His brows arched. "Why?"

"Because I'm going to massage some of those knots out of your shoulders." Very broad shoulders that sometimes carried too much weight.

"Jessie, I'm fine."

She pointed again. "Sit."

A smile curved his lips. "Where's Lisa?"

"Outside with Marly and Shannon setting up the croquet course. Ted's watching the hot dogs and hamburgers. Now, are you going to sit on the hassock, or do I have to stand on it to reach you?"

His smile broke into a grin, and he lowered himself to the hassock. Jessie stepped behind him, almost overwhelmed by the tenderness that washed over her for this man. He still hadn't told her why he'd become a doctor, where his dedication came from.

His black hair, slightly longer than when he'd arrived in Four Oaks, brushed his nape. The sudden longing to run her fingers through it shook Jessie. Laying her hands on his shoulders, she absorbed the sensations of cotton and male muscle underneath, which was indeed knotted. She slid her thumbs from his neck to his shoulders, testing, gently soothing, smoothing. He dropped his head with a low groan of pleasure.

Not only his shoulder muscles were tense, but his neck muscles, too. It gave her an excuse to slip her fingers into his hair, to caress his neck with her fingertips.

"You have magic hands," he said in a low, husky murmur.

The impulse to kiss the nape of his neck was so strong, she closed her eyes. Feelings from long ago toppled over feelings she had for him now....

Now.

She did have feelings for Gavin now. And they were just as strong as what she'd felt nine years ago. Standing with him like this, the desire as strong as ever, the want surprising her with its ache, she wondered how she'd ever denied them.

Opening her eyes, she moved her hands from his neck, where tender temptation was too strong, back to his shoulders. She leaned closer again—to inhale his scent . . . to remember.

Suddenly one of his large hands covered hers. "Jessie."

He turned his head, and the longing in his eyes told her he remembered, too.

Had she really been more than a passing fancy to him? When she'd made love with him, she'd given her love and every bit of her heart. Could she really believe he'd let her alone all these years so he'd have something to offer her? It didn't make sense to her when all she'd cared about was his love.

Suddenly the back screen door slammed. Lisa came running in. "Hey, Mom. Can we—? Dr. Bradley! You're here. Now we can eat."

Gavin took his hand from Jessie's. "And what's on the menu?"

Jessie was glad he'd asked a mundane question so she could regain her equilibrium.

"Hot dogs and hamburgers," Lisa answered, looking from Jessie to Gavin. "Is everything okay?"

Jessie moved then, away from Gavin, away from the feelings that caused nothing but chaos. "Everything's fine. Dr. Bradley is worried about a patient. He might have to go back to the hospital."

"Are we still going to the fireworks?" the eight-year-old asked hopefully.

Jessie put her arm around her daughter as Gavin rose from the hassock. "Sure. If Dr. Bradley has to leave, we can ride back with Marly. Now, come on, let's get this picnic underway or we won't have time for croquet before we go."

When she glanced at Gavin, he was frowning. She didn't know if it was meant for her or the world in general. But as her gaze collided with his, she knew something was on his mind—it had been since that day at his friend's cabin. She sensed soon he'd want to talk about it . . . and about them.

* * *

The powers-that-be in Four Oaks counted the fireworks display as one of the year's most important events, Gavin had heard. But the white-and-blue-and-red fireworks bursting in the sky acted merely as a distraction as he sat on a blanket next to Jessie, mindful of his daughter standing with Marly only a few feet away. He was trying his damnedest not to push Jessie, not to let a kiss or a touch go too far as they had at the cabin.

He'd also been wrestling with the questions Jessie had asked him that day. He'd thought his past was behind him and couldn't touch him now, but how would Jessie react to his background? The same way as her father? Did breeding matter to her as it mattered to Owen Windsor?

Until that Sunday at the cabin, Gavin had never realized how ashamed he was of the life he'd come from—a father who was drunk more often than he was sober, who'd taken his bottle with him to an early grave. At times Gavin had hated the man who was too weak to get help or to even care about the next day or a life beyond the tenement building.

Although she'd been illiterate, Gavin had always admired his mother. She'd brought as much good to their lives as she could working in a factory day after day, coming home to the squalor his father had helped create. She'd taught Gavin to dream about a better life. He'd done more than dream. But he'd lost her before he could make a difference in her life, too.

The crowd cheered and clapped as three white starbursts lit the sky simultaneously. Out of the corner of his eye, Gavin glimpsed a flurry of activity where Lisa stood.

Pushing himself up off his elbows, he sat up. An older child beside Lisa handed her a sparkler, a thin, rodlike stick that, when lit from the top, threw off sparks of fire. Lisa was holding it too close. A spark hit her knit top, and she jumped as one stung her leg.

Gavin was on his feet, beside her in a flash, reacting rather than thinking. He snatched the sparkler from her, stamping it out under his foot. Then he crouched down, holding her at the waist, his gaze scanning her for possible injury. "Don't ever play with anything like that again. Do you hear?" His voice was rough and harsh.

Jessie hunkered down beside Gavin. "Honey, are you okay?"

Shannon, Ted and Marly had gathered around her.

Lisa's eyes were wide, and her lower lip quivered. "Just my knee stings a little."

Gavin scooped her up. "I have my bag in the car. We'll put something on it."

"But the fireworks..."

"You can see them from the car. We'll come back here when we're done."

Lisa didn't argue with him, and neither did Jessie.

Jessie followed Gavin to his car. Lisa had looked so scared, Jessie didn't have the heart to scold her. Children thought they were indestructible, that no harm could come to them. Jessie knew better, and so did Gavin.

At the car, he examined Lisa's knee as she sat on the back seat with the car door open. Gently cleaning her knee with an antiseptic wipe, he then applied a salve. He didn't talk while he did it. Afterward he closed his bag. The car light illuminated Lisa's face as she looked up at him. "Dr. Bradley, please don't be mad at me."

The stiff line of his jaw softened. "I'm not angry with you. I guess I'm angry at myself for not watching you more closely."

Lisa hopped off the back seat. "Mom told me not to play with fireworks, but that boy just handed it to me...."

Jessie gave her daughter a hug. "Okay, it's over. It's forgotten. Do you want to just stay here and watch the rest? I think they're almost over."

Lisa nodded.

As Jessie and Gavin leaned against the car, Lisa sat and watched from the hood. Gavin was silent, and his silence made Jessie uneasy. On the drive home, she could see the tension in the straightness of his shoulders, the set of his jaw.

When he walked Jessie and Lisa to the door, he said, "I want to talk to you after you put Lisa to bed."

Once inside the house, Lisa looked up at him with an uncertain smile. "You're not still mad?"

He put his arms around her and gave her a long hug. "I'm not mad." Leaning away, he tipped her chin up. "You go to bed and have wonderful dreams. I'll see you soon."

With a sleepy smile, Lisa hugged him again, then went up the stairs. Jessie followed, trying to keep her heart from racing, trying to keep her jumbled nerves in line.

Lisa was too sleepy from the activities and excitement of the day to stall bedtime, so Jessie descended the steps to the living room about ten minutes later. Gavin was pacing, and she suddenly wanted to postpone whatever was coming. "Would you like something to drink?"

He stopped and faced her. "No. What I want is to tell Lisa I'm her father."

Chapter Eight

Jessie had expected this day to come. She just hadn't expected it to come so soon.

"I have to tell her, Jessie," Gavin said with a determination she was coming to know all too well. "Tonight when I saw her with that sparkler..." He shook his head. "I want to protect her, care for her, be involved in every decision that affects her. And I will be eventually, one way or the other."

"Whether I agree or not?" Suddenly his words clicked, and a terrible thought hit her. "You aren't thinking about suing for custody are you?"

Gavin stood tall, straight and imposing before her. His voice was iron hard, as hard as his eyes. "I would never do that to you. And the fact that you think I would makes me wonder if you and I have made any progress at all. It also means you have to make some decisions."

"What decisions?"

"Whether or not you're going to let me not only into Lisa's life, but into yours. I want more than co-parenting, more than friendship. Now you have to decide what you want."

"Gavin, you're acting as if this is black-and-white, as easy as making a decision. I don't *know* you anymore. I don't know if I *ever* knew you."

"What is it, Jessie? Are you like your father? Must you know about my breeding to know *me?* All right, I'll tell you. I grew up in a tenement in Richmond. My father was an alcoholic who couldn't hold a job more than a day and who drank himself to death. My mother couldn't read. She worked in a factory to put food on the table before *and* after he died. She was a proud woman and wouldn't take handouts, let alone welfare. Because of that, we never had health insurance. When I was away at school, she got a cold. It developed into pneumonia. She died."

Gavin raked his hand through his hair, and the muscles in his jaw worked. "You asked why I became a doctor. I saw pregnant teenagers not getting care for their unborn children. I saw babies and children who needed a simple antibiotic, suffering because they didn't have it. I saw my mother not go to the doctor so she could feed us. I couldn't help everyone, so I decided to help the children. I will never turn a child away because the parents can't pay."

"Gavin..."

"I don't want your pity, Jessie. This is who I am. I *am* going to tell Lisa I'm her father. What you need to decide is whether we're going to set up formal visitation rights or whether you want me to be more than Lisa's father. I know I've just given you a lot to sort through. Call me when you've made a decision. Call me when you know what you feel."

What she felt? She felt as if her world were spinning and she didn't know how to stop it. She felt as if Gavin had just issued an ultimatum, and she was too frozen to react.

When she didn't respond right away, Gavin's mouth straightened into a taut line. "I know what *I* want, Jessie. I want back what we had nine years ago and I want more. Now it's up to you."

With a last long, probing look, he turned and left her house. Maybe her life.

A week later, Gavin sat in his office across from Patti Rogers and finished another quarter of the club sandwich he'd brought up from the cafeteria. She absently munched on a french fry that had been nestled against the tuna sandwich she hadn't yet touched because she was too busy jotting down notes on some special programs he'd like to incorporate into pediatrics—one in particular was a Saturday-afternoon entertainment hour. He'd like to find volunteers to read to the kids, do magic tricks, maybe bring in pets—anything to make a hospital stay more palatable. Gavin believed attitude had much to do with healing.

Healing.

All of his thoughts took him back to Jessie. It had been a week since he'd left her so abruptly. The turmoil inside him had been building since their day at Jeff and Katie's cabin. He couldn't be around Jessie and not want to kiss her, touch her, make love to her. He couldn't be around Lisa and not want the three of them to be a family.

Maybe he'd wanted to shake Jessie up. But he might have shaken too hard. Or maybe…she thought like her father. Maybe no matter what he accomplished, he wouldn't be worthy in her eyes. Or maybe she'd never forgive him for leaving her nine years ago.

"Gavin?"

He looked across the desk at Patti and realized she'd probably said something besides his name and he hadn't heard.

"You're a million miles away."

"No, not that far." Five miles away. Thinking about Jessie and Lisa settling in for the evening, wondering if he'd screwed things up big-time.

"Do you want to do this another time?"

"No. I want to get the program implemented. Do you think we'll have any problems with the board passing it?"

"Not if it doesn't cost them any money," she said in a wry tone.

He laughed. "What a cynic."

She arched a brow and picked up half of her tuna sandwich. When she took a bite, some of it spilled onto the desk and her lap.

"Here, let me help." Gavin leaned forward with the napkins.

* * *

Inhaling a deep breath, Jessie opened the door to Gavin's office and stepped into the waiting room. It was empty. So was the receptionist's chair behind the glass window. Good. They'd have privacy.

She'd wanted to face Gavin, not call him. Most days, after he'd seen his last patient, he caught up on notes or dictation in his office. Since the waiting-room door was still unlocked, that's where she expected him to be now.

When he'd walked out of her house on the Fourth of July, she'd been numb. Questions had sped through her mind—should she give Gavin visitation rights? Is that what she wanted? What would Lisa's reaction be? What was the best way to tell her Gavin was her father?

Jessie had let the questions tumble over each other, angry with Gavin for backing her into a corner. Until she finally realized she'd backed him into a corner, too. How could he be a parent without his child knowing he was her father?

Jessie had thought about everything he'd said, especially the way he'd grown up. She admired him. Did he really think his background would make a difference to her? It was when she'd asked herself that question that she'd let the feelings come—past feelings and present feelings. She'd never gotten involved with another man because of Gavin. Yes, she'd been afraid of getting hurt again. But in her heart, she'd also known she'd never feel that deeply again.

She'd thought and felt and weighed until she was exhausted by all of it. And this morning she'd awakened knowing she wanted to try again with Gavin; she wanted Lisa to know he was her father.

Nervous but sure of her decision, Jessie pulled open the door leading to the hall of examination rooms and Gavin's office.

She heard a soft voice, then Gavin's deep laugh. Maybe his receptionist hadn't left. Maybe... Reaching his office before she analyzed further, she stopped short, impressions hitting her. Patti Rogers and Gavin—talking and laughing, in his office, after hours. Sandwiches, drinks, conversation. Gavin leaning across to Patti—

She must have made a sound, because two heads swung toward her. Gavin's gaze smacked into hers, and she knew there was no way she could hide her thoughts or the hurt. Jessie stepped back quickly, feeling much too vulnerable to say anything but "I'm... I'm sorry I interrupted."

Then she turned and fled down the hall, into the reception area, out the door. She thought Gavin called her name, but she wasn't sure. And she wasn't stopping to find out.

Gavin drove to Jessie's town house, definitely driving above the speed limit. When he had looked up, had seen Jessie in the doorway and the stunned expression on her face, he'd known exactly what she was thinking. And when she took off down the hall, he'd let out a string of epithets that had made Patti

Rogers blush. He'd called Jessie's name, but by the time he'd reached the waiting room, she was gone.

He'd been tempted to race out to the parking lot, but he didn't want a public confrontation. He wanted to talk to her in private, find out why she'd come to his office and why she'd reacted so strongly. To him, it meant she still cared . . . a lot. All he had to do was get her to admit it.

When he'd returned to his office, he'd been short with Patti. That wasn't fair. The whole situation wasn't her fault; it wasn't anybody's fault. It was a misunderstanding he was going to straighten out right now.

He parked the car in Jessie's driveway and strode up to the house. When he rang the doorbell, he wasn't surprised that she didn't answer. The town house was dark except for the dim glow of a light upstairs. Ringing the doorbell repeatedly, he muttered a few more choice words.

Not intending to wait to settle the misunderstanding, he went around to the back and saw the light shining in the room over the patio. He picked up a few stones he found in the flower bed and tossed them up at the open window. They pinged against the screen. When he got no response, he aimed higher and hit the glass. He saw a shadow, then Jessie's profile.

"I'm not leaving, Jessie, till we talk." Met with silence, frustrated, he called, "If you don't open the door, I'll climb up the awning and pound on your window until you let me in. I'm *not* leaving."

Finally she stooped down at the screen. "And what if I call the police?"

"I don't think you want to see the father of your child carted off in handcuffs or be the center of the commotion it would cause."

"That's blackmail."

"Deal with it," he retorted, his patience running thin.

Finally she said, "All right. I'll be right down."

Gavin felt as if he'd at least won the battle when the light went on in the kitchen and Jessie unlocked the door. But one look into her turmoiled blue eyes convinced him he had a long way to go.

He opened the screen door and stepped inside. As he did, Jessie stepped away and fortified herself behind a kitchen chair. "Where's Lisa?" he asked calmly.

"She's with the Millers. Ted had the day off and took them to a water-slide park. They'll probably be back anytime."

Silence stretched between them as Gavin tried to decide the best way to approach this. "Why did you come to my office tonight?"

"It doesn't . . . m-matter."

Frustrated with her, as well as with fate, he crossed to her and held her shoulders. "Tell me."

Tears welled up in her eyes. "There's no p-point. . . ." At the struggle to get the word out, her eyes grew wide, and she put her hand over her mouth, turning away from him.

"Jessie, what's wrong?"

She kept turned away and shook her head. "I c-can't..." Then she clamped her lips shut and pulled out of his grasp.

Suddenly he understood. Apparently Jessie had become a speech therapist for a very personal reason. He walked up behind her and clasped her shoulder. "You don't have to hide from me, Jessie."

She turned around and faced him, anger blazing in her blue eyes. After several deep breaths, she said, "The last time I stuttered, I was a teenager!"

Gavin had read up on the problem before he'd consulted with Jessie about Rodney. "And why did it happen now?"

Tears ran down her cheeks. "B-because I care too much about you and what we meant to each other and..."

He didn't wait for more but took her into his arms and crushed his mouth on hers. At first she resisted, the anger still in evidence. But as he laced his fingers into her hair and held her, letting her know he cared just as much, the resistance vanished. Her rigid body became pliant, and he slid his hands down her back, plunging his tongue into her mouth, kissing her as he wanted to kiss her every time he saw her.

But as abruptly as she'd melted against him, she broke the kiss and pulled away. "How can you kiss me like that when just a little while ago you were—" She stopped.

"Finish it, Jessie. What was I doing?"

She backed up against the counter. "You were flirting with Patti Rogers. You were just about—"

"To wipe the tuna fish she'd spilled off the desk," he cut in before Jessie could put anything else into words.

"Tuna fish," she said flatly.

"Yes, tuna fish. It's still sitting in my office because I left before I cleaned it up. Patti and I were going over ideas for the entertainment hour I want to start in the pediatrics ward every Saturday. As special-programs director, she'll present the concept to the board."

Jessie's face grew rosy. "I thought you'd decided to go on with your life because I took too long. I thought..."

He caressed her cheek. "You thought *wrong*. There is nothing between me and Patti Rogers. Now tell me why you came to my office," he urged gently.

"I came b-because..."

He could see the depth of her feelings was causing her stuttering. "It's okay, Jessie."

She took a measured breath. "I came because I want to try again. I want to tell Lisa you're her father."

At last after all his hoping and praying... Taking Jessie into his arms, he held her. Just as he leaned away and lowered his lips to hers, he heard a car, then slamming doors. His daughter was home.

Jessie leaned back and asked, "Do you want to help tuck her in? If she's not too tired, we can tell her."

His throat tightened. "Yes." He was finally going to claim his daughter and a future for which he'd worked nine long years.

* * *

Lisa ran in the back door and stopped when she saw Gavin. Her face lit up. "Hi, Dr. Bradley."

Shannon came to the screen. "Just wanted to make sure she got in okay."

Going to the door Jessie asked her neighbor, "Did you have a nice day?"

"We had a great day. Next time you'll have to come along." Shannon threw a look toward Gavin and raised her brows. In a low voice, she asked, "Do you want Lisa to stay over with Marly?"

Jessie shook her head. "No. I'll tell you why tomorrow. Or Lisa will."

Shannon shook her finger at her friend. "You'd better tell me. Or I'll encourage the girls to have a pajama party at your house with at least ten of their friends."

Jessie smiled and waited until Shannon reached her own patio before she switched off the porch light.

Crossing to her daughter, who was telling Gavin about the water slides, Jessie put an arm around her. "Let's go get you a shower and get ready for bed."

"Aw, Mom..."

"After you're in your pj's, Dr. Bradley and I want to talk to you about something."

Lisa looked from Jessie to Gavin. "Are you gonna be boyfriend and girlfriend?"

Gavin smiled. "That's a good possibility. But there's more, too. After your shower, we'll have a powwow."

Gavin's encouragement got Lisa moving. She took the fastest shower in her young history and impatiently fidgeted while Jessie dried her hair. Finally, with her hair fluffy and soft, her cheeks still rosy from her shower, she climbed into her bed and waited expectantly.

After straightening the pink-flowered spread on her daughter's bed, Jessie sat on one side of Lisa, Gavin on the other. She wasn't sure how to begin or the best way to break the news.

Gavin took Jessie's hand. "Lisa, your mom and I knew each other a long time ago when we were in college."

Lisa's eyes grew wide. "You did?"

Jessie nodded. "But then Gavin went away to medical school."

"A short time later," he continued, "your mom found out she was pregnant...with you. Because she thought I didn't care about her anymore, she didn't tell me. But when I came to Four Oaks and saw you, I figured it out. So what we're trying to tell you in a roundabout way is that I'm your dad."

Jessie could feel the tension in Gavin's hand as he waited for Lisa's response.

She looked from one of them to the other. "Now I have a dad like everyone else?"

"You've always had a dad," Jessie answered gently. "You just didn't know him. Now you do."

Suddenly a smile bloomed, growing bigger and wider, then Lisa was on her knees with her arms around Gavin's neck.

Jessie saw the moisture in his eyes as he let go of her hand and hugged his daughter. His voice was husky when he asked, "Does this mean you're happy about it?"

Lisa released him and sat back on her heels. "You're the best. Can I call you Dad?"

"You sure can." He ruffled her hair affectionately.

Switching her attention to Jessie, Lisa asked, "Is he going to move in with us?"

Jessie swallowed hard and thought before she answered. "Your dad and I are getting to know each other again. So for now, things will stay as they are."

Lisa seemed to accept that, though the heated gaze Gavin threw Jessie made her wonder what he was thinking.

"Can we do family stuff like Marly and her mom and dad do?"

"What kind of family stuff?" Gavin asked.

"Like going to the water-slide park?"

Gavin grinned. "We'll try to fit that in. I have a couple of things in mind myself, but I want to talk to your mom about them." He stood, then leaned over and gave Lisa a kiss on the forehead. "We'll have plenty of time to talk about all this. For now, I think it's bedtime."

Lisa sighed. "You're gonna be just like Mom, aren't you?"

He chuckled. "Is that so bad?"

Looking at Jessie, Lisa smiled. "Nope."

Jessie hugged and kissed Lisa, then turned off the light. "Honey, if you have any questions about me and your dad, we'll try to answer them."

"Okay, Mom. G'night."

"'Night. Sweet dreams."

Jessie preceded Gavin down the stairs but could feel his gaze on her all the way to the living room.

At the bottom of the steps, he caught her arm. When he tugged her into his embrace, she went willingly. His lips sought hers, and she could feel all the emotion that had been building inside both of them. It exploded into a kiss that made the Fourth of July fireworks seem like just a flicker. His tongue eagerly stroked hers, and the fiery response he evoked urged her to hold on to him tighter, to believe in their future, to throw all her doubts aside. Yet she couldn't quite do that. Her heart told her to give him everything she was, everything she had. But another voice cautioned her not to rush, to make sure this time.

As if Gavin sensed the boundary she'd drawn, he pulled back. Caressing her cheek, he said, "I think Lisa's idea of doing 'family stuff' is a good one. Jeff and Katie are having a christening for their daughter in two weeks in D.C. You and Lisa are invited. What do you think?"

"You can get away?"

"I'll find someone to cover. Cade and Randi will be there. I'd like you meet them."

"And Nathan?"

"Nathan, too."

These friends of Gavin's were his extended family. She wanted to meet them. "I'd like to go."

He tilted her chin up. "I've waited for you for nine years. I'm not going to rush you into anything. This time we'll do it right."

Jessie closed her eyes as Gavin bent his head to kiss her again. Yes, this time she'd do it right.

Chapter Nine

As Lisa splashed in Owen Windsor's pool one hot, end-of-July evening, Jessie decided to broach the subject of Gavin with her father. It had only been a week since she and Gavin had told Lisa the truth about Gavin. In that week, he'd stopped in several nights. As he'd promised, he wasn't pushing, but every time she saw him interact with Lisa, talk with her, hug her, listen to her, Jessie realized his dedication to being a father was as strong as his dedication to his profession. And each time he kissed Jessie or touched her, she realized the future held more promise than she ever believed it could.

Knowing she couldn't put it off any longer, Jessie said, "Lisa knows Gavin is her father."

"I know," Owen snapped, laying the evening newspaper on his lap. "She couldn't wait to tell me when she came in. You were getting her duffel bag out of the car. I wondered when *you* were going to tell me."

Jessie heard the note of disapproval she knew so well. "She's happy about it."

Owen scowled. "She might be happy now. What if he doesn't stick around—like before?"

"He's a wonderful father. She loves spending time with him. He has no intention of leaving."

"Has Peter Winnichuk decided to retire?" Owen asked, his brows in their inquisition mode.

"I don't know. Have you heard something?"

"No. And that's the point. Bradley is only taking over temporarily. Then what?"

She and Gavin hadn't talked about the future—they were trying to establish the present. "Dad, Gavin is here to stay. When are you going to accept him as part of my life?"

Her father shifted in the outdoor chair. "When I see it's inevitable. I'm not sure it is yet."

"Why are you so doubtful?"

"Past history," he said gruffly. "Gavin Bradley and your mother are..."

"Are what?"

He looked away. "I just don't want to see you and Lisa hurt like I was when your mother left...like you were. Be careful, Jessie."

"I am being careful."

After a doubtful grunt, he asked, "Has Bradley said anything to you about me?"

"Like what?" she asked cautiously.

Her father studied her face. "Never mind. It doesn't matter."

"It would be nice if you asked Gavin to Sunday dinner."

"I'm not ready to do that yet," her father muttered.

"But you'll think about it?" she pressed.

His gaze met hers. "I'll think about it."

Jessie smiled. Progress. A little at a time. Her father would like Gavin if he got to know him—she knew he would. Soon they'd all really be a family.

Jeff Stanhope proudly stood by his wife, Katie, at the church's altar as she held their baby daughter after the christening. "Let's go out on the steps so everyone can get all the pictures they want," he suggested. "Then on back to our place. You can change into comfortable clothes again."

Still standing in one of the pews, Gavin curled his arm around Jessie's shoulders and took a deep breath, wondering if he'd ever been as happy as he was at this moment. Here, among friends, with Jessie and their daughter, he felt as if finally everything was right with the world. As they'd stood, listening to the words of the christening ceremony, watching Jeff and Katie and their new baby, Gavin hoped for the same happiness for him and Jessie. With telling Lisa he was her father, with Jessie's enthusiasm for this trip, he felt as if that happiness could be within his grasp.

Leaning close to Jessie's ear, he asked, "Did I tell you how beautiful you look?" His gaze skimmed over her elegant rose dress and jacket, took in her tiny opal drop earrings, then came to rest on her lips.

She smiled. "I think right before we left for the church you said something about Lisa and I looking like models."

Beside him, Lisa tugged on Gavin's hand. "Gregory, Tim and Sean went outside. Can I?"

Lisa had gotten along well with Cade and Randi's three boys. But left to their own devices too long, they'd definitely get into mischief. "We'll come outside with you," Gavin answered with a smile.

Out on the church steps, first Katie and Jeff's family, then Cade, then other guests took pictures while the children squirmed and the hot sun beat down. Soon the men had thrown their suit jackets over their arms. As Randi and Jessie became involved in a conversation about working mothers while they kept an eye on their children, Cade slapped Gavin on the back.

"I almost dropped my fork at lunch when Lisa called you 'Dad'. You didn't know?"

"Not until after I got to Four Oaks."

Cade slanted his gaze toward his sons. "It's some responsibility, isn't it?"

"You should know. Like Jessie, you did it on your own."

Cade's gaze found his wife. "But not anymore. I can't imagine how I did it without Randi."

Gavin chuckled. "Why do I get the feeling you two are still on your honeymoon?"

Cade reluctantly pulled his attention from his pretty, auburn-haired wife. "I intend to be for a long time. What about you? When are you and Jessie going to tie the knot?''

Gavin wanted nothing more than to get married as soon as possible. But he knew Jessie needed more time.

"Problems on your side or hers?" Once a stockbroker, now a Montana rancher, Cade had always possessed the ability to read people well.

"Hers. She's holding back. And I'm not sure she knows it."

Flipping his Western-cut suit jacket over his shoulder on a crooked finger, Cade said, "You know the problems I had giving the last inch."

"The last inch?" Gavin asked knowingly. Cade had been a bear in pain before he'd finally laid his pride aside and given in to his love for Randi.

Ignoring the friendly jibe, Cade asked, "Are you planning to stay in Four Oaks?"

Gavin thought about the job offer he'd received last week. Before he'd decided to come to Four Oaks, he'd sent his credentials and résumé to a pediatrician in Denver who studied developmental problems in children. Last week the doctor had invited him to work on his team. But Gavin now knew he wanted a practice and life with Jessie and Lisa in Four Oaks more than he ever wanted to work on a special project.

He answered Cade's question with a sureness he felt in his heart. "Yes, I plan to stay in Four Oaks."

Cade studied him for a moment. "It boils down to trust. You and I both know that."

"Although I had good intentions, I broke that trust once. Sometimes I wonder what I'll have to do to fix it."

"You love her, don't you?"

"I've loved her for nine years."

"Then just keep showing her. She'll get it eventually."

Gavin wanted to believe his friend was right. But he wasn't so sure. Jessie's upbringing made trust difficult for her. Gavin hadn't had much, but he'd always known the power of his mother's love. He just wished Jessie would open herself up to the power of *his* love.

Sipping a glass of iced tea, Jessie watched as Gavin and Cade play dodge ball with Tim, Gregory, Sean and Lisa. Most of the guests had left or gone inside, where the air-conditioning cooled off the high-eighties temperature.

She heard the sliding glass door open and close and turned to watch Nathan Maxwell sink into the lawn chair beside her.

"How long are you staying?" he asked.

"Until around five." With all the guests milling about, she and Nathan hadn't had much opportunity to talk. "I was sorry you couldn't drive up with us."

"I'm spending a few days with friends in the area."

Jessie nodded. "Gavin told me. After you get back, maybe we can all get together some evening."

Nathan looked surprised and then he smiled. "I'd like that."

Jessie had always liked Nathan. She knew Gavin wanted to renew his friendship with him.

After a few moments of silence, Nathan said, "I've been watching Gavin with Lisa today. He likes being a father."

Jessie knew anyone could see it. "He's a great father."

"Do you like him *being* her father?"

When she'd met Nathan nine years ago, one of the qualities she'd admired about him was his candor. "Yes, I do. At first I was worried his dedication to his profession wouldn't leave him enough time for her. But he makes the time. And more important, when he's with her, she has all his attention."

"I don't know if I've ever admired anyone the way I admire Gavin," Nathan mused, stretching his long legs out in front of him. "What he came from, what he's accomplished, the determination and work it's taken to get him there. Now I hope he can just enjoy it."

"What do you mean?" She set her iced tea on the patio.

"Has he told you how he grew up?"

She nodded.

"Because of his background, he's always felt he had something to prove. I don't know if he realizes he doesn't have anything to prove anymore."

The dodge-ball game broke up, and Jessie stood. Amid the children's complaints of "I'm thirsty," Gavin curled his arm around Jessie's waist. "We better get on the road."

"I know." She heard the wistfulness in her voice, and so did Gavin.

He kissed her temple as if it was the most natural gesture in the world even in the midst of his friends. She realized she wasn't embarrassed; she liked belonging with Gavin.

With a gentle hug, he asked, "What's wrong?"

She shook her head. "Absolutely nothing. I loved being here with you this weekend."

Smiling warmly, he enveloped her in a huge bear hug. She was exactly where she wanted to be.

The following morning, an impatient Jessie stepped inside her father's office. "What was so urgent, Dad, that you couldn't tell me on the phone?" She glanced at her watch. "I have a half hour before I have to be back for my next appointment."

"Sit down, Jessica. I have something to tell you."

Goose bumps broke out on her arms, and a sense of foreboding led her to the chair in front of her father's desk. "What's wrong?"

As she sat, so did her father, but he leaned forward, his forehead creased, his expression grim. "Once again my instincts were correct. Lack of breeding shows. It was true of your mother and it's true of Gavin Bradley."

"Lack of breeding? I don't understand. You mentioned Gavin and my mother before. There's no connection."

"Oh, yes, there is, Jessica. Your mother's father had been in and out of jail all her life. Her mother only finished high school. I took her away from all that. I couldn't help myself. She seemed so delicate...she was so beautiful...." He paused. "But her background had made her selfish. She didn't care about anyone else. She used me and my money and then she left, chasing a passion she said we never had. When I told her you were staying with me, that she'd have to go to court if she wanted visitation rights, she didn't even put up a fight. We meant nothing to her, Jessica."

Jessie swallowed the old hurt, the knowledge that her mother hadn't wanted her.

"It was the way she was raised—no sense of loyalty, no sense of commitment. I was so caught up in her outside beauty...the idea I could change her..." He shook his head. "And Gavin Bradley is no different. He has always looked out for himself."

"You don't *know* him!"

"I know his kind. When you were so enamored with him in college, I investigated him. His father was an alcoholic, his mother illiterate—"

"I know Gavin's background," she cut in. "He told me."

"Did he also tell you the reason he never contacted you?"

"He said he didn't feel he had anything to offer me, that he didn't want me to sacrifice—"

"Hogwash! I told him I'd see to it he never got his medical degree if he didn't stay away from you."

"You did what?"

"You heard me. His career was more important to him than you ever were. And now it's going to be again. Has he told you he's been offered a position in Denver?''

Jessie was having trouble assimilating everything her father had told her—about her mother, about obviously meeting Gavin nine years ago, about what was happening now. "No, he hasn't. How do you know about it?''

"As chairman of the hospital board, I make it my business to know. He received the offer over a week ago.''

Why hadn't Gavin told her? *Was* he considering it? Certainly he couldn't think she'd yank Lisa away from everything familiar. But then again, maybe he wasn't considering her or Lisa at all. Maybe this position in Denver was a stepping-stone. She remembered what Nathan had said about Gavin having something to prove. Maybe she and Lisa weren't enough for him. And if her father was right about why Gavin had stayed away from her nine years ago...

Her hands were shaking, and as she stood, she realized her whole body shook. She needed time alone. She needed time to think. No, she needed to see Gavin. Now.

Knowing that at midmorning, Gavin usually made his rounds at the hospital, Jessie took the elevator to the pediatrics ward.

She walked down the tiled floor, her hands clammy as she glanced in the rooms and listened for Gavin's voice. Her heart thumped faster than she walked, and she realized she was almost afraid to find him and ask the questions that had to be asked. But fear wouldn't stop her. Long ago she'd found the way to win over fear was to face it head-on.

Still . . .

So many thoughts ran through her mind. Why had neither Gavin nor her father told her about their confrontation nine years ago? If they hadn't told her about that, what else hadn't they told her? Had Gavin really come to Four Oaks because of her? He was so good with Lisa, but just how deep was his commitment to his daughter? Would he leave her behind to further his career?

And then there was the toughest question of all. Was Gavin in love with her? Or had she been deluding herself again? Reading love into words and kisses when it wasn't there?

She found Gavin in the room at the end of the hall. He sat on a chair by one of the beds. The second bed was empty. The boy was hardly a child—he looked more like a teenager. She remembered Gavin's concern for the child in intensive care on the Fourth of July, the many pages he answered, the calls he made to check on patients.

His voice was concerned now as he said to the teenager, "There will be other seasons."

"You don't understand, Dr. Bradley. Being quarterback is everything. The coach will never let me play if I miss preseason training. Can't I push it? Can't I . . ."

"Devon, your body needs time to heal. If you rush it, you know you'll leave yourself open to injury. I won't okay you getting back to training until I'm sure you're ready.''

''I'll get another doctor,'' the boy muttered.

''You could do that. But a few weeks isn't a lifetime. And there will be other seasons. There's no saying that once you are ready to go back, you can't catch up. Talk to your coach. If you want me to talk to him, I will.'' He stood and clapped the teenager on the shoulder. ''I'll stop in again later.''

Devon raised his head. ''Maybe I can run some plays by you.''

Gavin smiled. ''Have them ready.''

When Gavin turned and saw Jessie, his smile widened. ''Did you come over to share cafeteria food with me?''

''No. Gavin, I have to talk to you. Can we go to your office?''

He searched her face. ''Is there a problem with Lisa?''

''No, but I have to talk to you in private.''

''I just have to drop this chart at the desk. Let's go.''

Jessie couldn't make small talk in the elevator, not with all the questions clicking through her mind. Gavin didn't speak, either, and she wondered if he suspected what she'd discovered. He unlocked the door to his offices and held it open while she stepped inside. Her arm brushed his suit jacket. His scent tempted her to bury herself in his arms and forget what her father had told her. But she couldn't. She needed answers.

In his office, Gavin sat on a corner of the desk. "Okay, shoot. What's going on?"

"I just came from my father."

Gavin's jaw set; his eyes lost their warmth. "And?"

"Why didn't you tell me you met him nine years ago? Why didn't you tell me he threatened you?"

"Is that what he told you?"

"He told me that he warned you to stay away from me and if you didn't, he'd prevent you from getting your medical degree."

"Do you believe that's why I never called you?"

"Is it the truth?"

"It's true your father tried to intimidate me. It's true that he made me look at reality from his perspective. I was young, poor, no family, no money, deep in debt. But I did write you a letter to explain."

"A letter I never received."

Gavin stood and came toward her and, as always when he wanted her full attention, he held her shoulders. "Do you believe I sent it?"

Jessie had never focused on that question, because in the scheme of things it had become unimportant... until now. She remembered the things her father had said and she had doubts.

Gavin saw them. He dropped his hands.

"Gavin, I want to believe you—"

"What if your father took it and destroyed it?"

"He wouldn't..."

Gavin gave a mirthless laugh. "One point that's incontrovertible is that your father came to me so he could meddle in your life. I never told you because I

didn't want to interfere in your relationship with him.
I figured it would backfire and come between us. But
your father doesn't have those qualms. He'll manipulate any situation if it will get him what he wants."

"He wants what's best for me and Lisa."

"If it's what *he* wants," Gavin repeated. "I'm not
going to stand here and tell you he's a manipulator,
because if you think about your past with him, you'll
realize he is."

"The past and my father have nothing to do with
the fact that you're considering a job offer in Denver
and didn't tell me about it."

"Where did you get this information?" Gavin
asked, his voice harder than she'd ever heard it.

"Are you saying it isn't true?" This time Jessie
hoped with all her heart her father was lying.

"I did receive an offer from a hospital in Denver
about a week ago."

"Are you considering it?"

"I considered it, and I didn't tell you about it because I only thought it over for five minutes and decided you and Lisa were more important and I was
staying right here. But now maybe I should question
what I decided."

She took a deep breath and asked, "Why?"

"I thought time was all we needed, Jessie. I
thought time would heal the wound. I thought in time
you'd forgive me for leaving, forgive me for deciding
I didn't want you to sacrifice *your* life the way I had
to sacrifice mine, for deciding I wanted to come to
you a man with something to offer. But now I don't
know if you're ever going to trust me. Without trust,

we'll never have anything to build on. Your father and his influence in your life seem to be more important than any love I could offer you."

"That's not fair," she cried, feeling Gavin slipping away and not knowing what to do about it.

"I think it's a more than fair assessment of everything that's happened since I came to Four Oaks. You told me we could try again, Jessie. What does that mean? How can we try again if you don't trust me?"

"I have to be sure this time. I have to—"

"If you don't trust me, Jessie, we don't have anything," he concluded, his voice rough.

"We have Lisa."

He shook his head. "I want more than Lisa. Sometime you're going to have to stop seeing yourself through your father's eyes—stop seeing the little girl whose mother didn't love her enough to stay, stop seeing the little girl who was so insecure about her father's love she stuttered. You have to realize you're a woman who can share love and give love and take love. Until you do see yourself that way, maybe all I can be is Lisa's father."

Gavin's words hurt because she knew they were true, just as she knew her doubts had damaged their relationship irrevocably.

"I don't think there's anything else to talk about, Jessie. Not until we *both* do some hard thinking."

Gavin had given her every opportunity to trust him, to depend on him, to love him. But now he was shutting her out.

She could tell by the guarded look in his eyes, the rigid set of his shoulders, his hands, which he'd clenched into fists. And she knew there was nothing she could say that would make everything right again.

She had to leave before she started crying. She had to leave before she begged for forgiveness. Because even if she begged, he wouldn't be able to forgive her now.

Turning, she hoped he'd call her name as he'd done so many times in the past two months. But he didn't call, he didn't move, he didn't blink. He just let her go.

Gavin swiped everything from his desk with a loud curse. He'd never been angrier—angry at Jessie, angry at fate, angry at her father. Maybe he should have trounced the man when he'd had the chance. But Gavin believed in playing fair. He'd thought by playing fair, he'd build bridges, not burn them. Well, Owen Windsor was out to burn bridges. Gavin's bridges. And now there was nothing more Owen Windsor could do. There was nothing more Gavin could do, either.

Nine long years he'd worked to prove he was worthy of Jessie Windsor's love. And now, by God, he was worthy. And if she couldn't accept that and accept him, then they didn't belong together.

Chapter Ten

Somehow Jessie got through the day, blocking what had happened as well as she could as she helped her clients, trying to control the emotions that flooded her when she wasn't engrossed in her work—emotions too numerous to count, too potent to ignore, too overwhelming to deny. Finally she realized how much she loved Gavin. She deeply regretted hurting him because of her doubts and fears.

Her father's messages came in one after the other on her answering machine. But she couldn't talk to him. She was too upset, too angry. She had to do some sorting before she could speak to him again. Right now she wanted to yell and scream, *Why didn't you mind your own business?* But she knew what his reply would be—she *was* his business.

Thankfully Lisa spent the evening on the front walk with her skateboard and Marly. Jessie picked up the phone to call Gavin at least ten times. But she knew Gavin needed more than words from her. What would it take to make amends? What would help him believe in their future again? Right now she was afraid he believed they didn't *have* a future. Tears welled up in her eyes over and over. What had she done?

She went over their conversation again and again, remembering every word. In essence, he'd told her her father was a master manipulator. As Gavin had directed, she thought about her history with her dad. He'd always been in control, out of reach, a power above her. She'd respected that power and she'd feared it. It wasn't his wealth or status that gave him power over her—it was his ability to withdraw from her when she didn't do what he wanted. He'd always seemed so far away.

He couldn't control his wife or keep her from leaving him, so he'd tried to control every aspect of Jessie's life, claiming he was looking after her interests. He'd chosen her extracurricular activities in high school the same way he'd tried to pick her friends. She'd learned trade-offs were a way of keeping peace. Because friends were important to her, she'd stood her ground on whom she spent time with. She gave in to him on activities and curfews. To avoid putting boys through an inquisition, she didn't date much but paid more attention to her studies—after all, good grades would make her father proud.

She'd chosen her major and let him pick the college. Although she lived her own life during the school year, she'd given in to his rules and regulations over the summers. She'd attended the country-club dances. But she'd always known she was waiting for someone special who could love her in a way she'd never been loved—unconditionally. Yes, her father had manipulated her life, and she'd let him because she'd never felt she had a choice.

Now she did.

Deep in her heart, she knew Gavin and his strength of character. Maybe her father had threatened him, but she believed now he'd sent her a letter, she believed now that he'd thought he was doing the best thing for her when he'd left for med school. He was a noble man. A good man. An unselfish man. But the realization had come too late.

Too late. Too late. Too late.

The words echoed over and over again as Jessie put Lisa to bed, as she turned down her own bed, as she switched off her bedside lamp. The tears kept coming, and finally she gave up trying to keep the dam from breaking. It was time she felt it all.

The following evening, Jessie was cleaning up the supper dishes when the doorbell rang. Hoping against hope that Gavin might be standing on the porch, she rushed to the living room. But she didn't find Gavin; she found her father.

He spoke to her through the screen. "You can't ignore me forever."

Ignoring him wasn't even a possibility. She was still trying to figure out how to deal with him. But maybe the time for a confrontation had arrived.

Noting Lisa riding her skateboard with Marly a few houses down the street, Jessie opened the door.

Her father stepped inside. "Tell me what happened. Is he going to take the job?"

Jessie's anger bubbled up and spilled over. "It's none of your business. My personal life will never be your business again. I will not stand by while you manipulate my life. And if you ever try to interfere in Lisa's, I will cut off all contact with you."

Her father looked astonished but only for a moment. "I'd like to see you try. If you do anything so foolhardy, you won't see a nickel of your inheritance."

Quick tears blurred Jessie's eyes. Her father had never really known her. He didn't know what made her heart sing or the values that guided her life. If he did, he couldn't just threaten her, thinking his money mattered to her. "Do you think I care about my inheritance when I've lost the only man I've ever loved?"

"So he *is* leaving," Owen Windsor snapped.

"He had no intention of leaving until I betrayed him by my doubts and lack of trust. I'd like to blame that on you, but I can't. *I'm* the one who really knows Gavin. *I'm* the one who should have realized long before now that he'd never lie to me or do anything to intentionally hurt me. Unlike you."

"I wasn't trying to hurt you. I was trying to protect you," her father almost shouted with an outrage she knew was genuine.

"Protection can hurt as much as it can help. If I had received Gavin's letter, if I had realized he cared about me as much as I cared about him, I would have contacted him somehow. I would have convinced him sharing years of hardship in love wouldn't have been a sacrifice for me. I would have told him of my pregnancy. You robbed Lisa of eight years of knowing her father's love!"

"Don't get maudlin on me, Jessica. You and Lisa have had a perfectly good life—"

"You'll never get it, will you? *Things* don't mean anything. Money can't keep a heart from breaking or mend it when it does. You of all people should know that."

"Gavin Bradley will leave you as your mother left me."

Jessie's fuse, always long with her father because she'd wanted his love more than she'd wanted anything, suddenly became short and ignited. "You're living in a time warp, Dad. You're living with a paranoia that has kept you from loving again. Do you feel so comfortable with the years of bitterness that you're afraid to let them go?"

"You expect me to forgive and forget what she did?"

"Maybe you'll never forget, but if you don't forgive, it will eat away at you and destroy your relationship with me and Lisa. You can't control me anymore, Dad, but if you choose, you can love me.

The fact is—I'm no longer going to base what I do in my life on whether you do or don't. I've hurt Gavin deeply with my distrust. All I care about is building a life with him. I don't know if that's possible now or—''

The screech of a car's brakes stopped Jessie cold. With a mother's sixth sense, chills broke out on her arms. But before she could run to the door, Marly was there, yelling for Jessie, screaming something about Lisa's skateboard rolling from the driveway into the street.

Jessie tore out of the house and across the curb, where a green car had skidded to a stop. Lisa lay on the asphalt, her helmet knocked a few feet away, her forehead bleeding, her arm twisted at an unnatural angle. Jessie knew she'd never forget the sight or the fear or the panic that made her heart hammer against her breast and shortened her breaths.

She knelt by her daughter. ''Lisa, honey, can you hear me?''

Lisa stayed deathly still, and the panic grabbed Jessie more completely.

Her father suddenly knelt at her elbow. ''I called 911. They're on their way.''

''Call Gavin. Please call Gavin. He'll know what to do.'' She must have repeated it a hundred times, a thousand times. He was the only one she'd trust with Lisa.

It seemed forever before she heard the wail of the ambulance siren. A few minutes later, she watched the paramedics slip the oxygen tube into her daughter's nose, run the IV and then load Lisa into the back of the ambulance. She didn't wait for anyone's permission but climbed in beside her daughter and held her hand.

Gavin sat in his office, dreading going home to the silence of his apartment and the clamor of his thoughts. Hoping Jessie would call—but knowing if she did, he didn't know what he'd say—he'd tried to keep his mind on everything else but the two of them.

He'd been tough on her...maybe too tough. He remembered what he'd told her a few weeks before: *If you have a question about me or what I do, come to me directly.* She had. And what had he done? He'd come down on her. Hard. Her doubts, her lack of trust, had suddenly frustrated him beyond the patience he'd practiced so carefully. If he didn't have her trust, he'd never have her love. Desire was no substitute.

If Jessie's father constantly interfered in their lives, how could they find true intimacy? Jessie needed to believe in herself, as much as she needed to believe in him and in them as a couple. She had to believe in herself and her decisions and judgments, whether her father approved or not. For the most part, she did. But when it came to matters of the heart...when it came to Gavin...

He loved Jessie. He'd always love Jessie. But one person loving and trusting wasn't enough.

Suddenly his pager went off. Checking the number, he saw it was the emergency room. He jabbed in the digits and identified himself.

The nurse's voice was brisk. "Dr. Bradley, we just got a call for you. Your daughter was in an accident. The ambulance will be here in a few minutes."

He went numb. For a moment, the room turned black. Then adrenaline pumped. "I'll be right there." He slammed down the phone and ran for the hall.

Jessie scrambled out of the ambulance. As the paramedics pushed Lisa's gurney through the sliding glass doors, she told everyone she passed, "I want Dr. Bradley. Now."

Fear shook her body, but she held on to Lisa's hand, praying, and murmured to her, "Your dad will be here. You're going to be fine, baby. I love you."

All at once, Gavin appeared at the head of the gurney. "What happened?"

His face was neutral, professional, but in his eyes, Jessie could see he was fighting the same fear and panic surging through her. "She was on her skateboard. She must have been going too fast and rode off the driveway into the street. I don't know if the car hit her or she hit the car. But she opened her eyes in the ambulance. That's a good sign, isn't it?" Jessie's voice caught, and the tears she'd been holding back surfaced.

Gavin said to the paramedics, "Take her to ER 1. Dr. Daniels is there waiting." Grasping Jessie by the shoulders, he agreed, "That's a very good sign. I want you to wait here. We have to examine her and probably run some tests. I'll let you know as soon as I know anything." Releasing her, he turned to go.

She caught his arm. "Gavin, I . . ." The tears over-flowed and coursed down her cheeks, but she man-aged to continue, "I know you'll take care of her."

He nodded. "I won't leave her side." Then he dis-appeared into the examination room.

Jessie sank onto a hard vinyl chair in the waiting area, knowing she had to stay out of the way but longing to be in the examination room with her daughter. What if there were internal injuries? What if she needed surgery?

"Jessica, how is she?"

When Jessie looked up, she saw her father. "I don't know yet. Gavin's with her."

Owen Windsor remained silent. Then he reached over and covered Jessie's hand with his. "She'll be all right. She has to be."

Jessie closed her eyes tight against the tears.

A moment later she felt her father's arm around her shoulders. She opened her eyes and saw regrets on his face . . . and love in his eyes.

"Jessica . . . I'm sorry."

Never in this lifetime had she expected an apology from her father. "I love Gavin, Dad. Nothing will change that. If he forgives me for doubting him, I can't let you interfere again. If you can't accept him . . . accept us, then you can't be part of our lives." When she finished, she thought her father might withdraw from her.

He kept his arm where it was. "And if I try not to interfere?"

She looked squarely at him, knowing she now saw herself through her own eyes—not her father's, knowing her heart wouldn't deceive her. "Then maybe we can all be a family."

Her father gave her a slight nod of his head.

They had a long way to go, but at least they had started.

Some time later, Gavin entered the waiting area. Seeing Owen Windsor beside Jessie, he frowned.

Jessie jumped up. "How is she?"

Gavin kept his voice cool and professional. "She's awake and alert. We examined her and did an MRI. She's one tough little cookie. She's bruised. And we have to set her arm and stitch up her forehead, but I think she's going to be fine. She's asking for you, so why don't you come in for a few minutes before we set her arm. I want to keep her in the hospital for a day or two for observation, just to make sure we haven't missed anything." Expecting a comment or two from Owen Windsor, he was surprised when he didn't get any.

Jessie turned to her father. "You don't have to stay. I can call you later."

"I'll wait. Until after she's settled in a room."

Gavin figured Owen Windsor was still trying to exert his control, to make sure his granddaughter received the best of care. As if Gavin wouldn't see to it.

Jessie started toward the examining room, and Gavin turned to follow.

"Bradley?"

Gavin didn't feel this was the time or place for a showdown. But before he could say that, Owen Windsor informed him, "I want you to know when

Lisa got hit, Jessie called for you. She didn't want anyone else to take care of her daughter. Remember that.''

Gavin waited for more, but it didn't come. For now, Lisa was his main concern. He left Owen in the waiting room, more anxious to get back to his daughter than to think about what Jessie's father had said or why he'd said it.

It was almost ten p.m. when Gavin pushed Lisa's gurney down the hall to her room in the pediatrics ward.

''Mommy's going to be in my room?'' Lisa asked, looking small and delicate against the sheets. Her blue eyes were huge, since the gauze over her stitches seemed to cover most of her forehead.

''Yep, she'll be waiting. Maybe your grandfather, too. How are you feeling?''

''Sleepy.''

''That's from the medication we gave you before we set your arm.'' Arriving at Lisa's room, Gavin pushed the gurney inside. Jessie and Owen Windsor stood at the window.

Jessie came over to Lisa, and Gavin saw the tears well in her eyes. ''Let me get her settled in bed, then you can sit with her.'' Gently he lifted his daughter to her bed. ''This is one brave little girl. She did a great job while Dr. Daniels set her arm and I sewed up the stitches.''

Jessie sat next to Lisa and gave her a hug, careful of her arm. ''You have to stay in the hospital for a day or two. Did your dad tell you?''

Lisa bobbed her head. Then she said, "I'm sorry I went in the street, Mom. I didn't mean to. I was going real fast..." Tears filled her eyes.

Owen came over to the bed and patted his granddaughter's leg. "Accidents happen. What's important is that you're going to be fine."

Jessie brushed Lisa's hair from her cheek. "Gavin, can I stay here with her tonight?"

The second bed in the room was empty. "I'll arrange it. I'll go tell the nurses at the desk and give them Lisa's chart."

As Gavin went to the desk, gave instructions and made arrangements, fatigue set in. He knew it was more than a physical response to a long day. On the way back to Lisa's room, he passed Owen Windsor.

Owen stopped. "Thank you for taking care of Lisa the way you did."

Gavin said simply, "She's my daughter."

Owen looked as if he wanted to say something else, but he didn't. He nodded and continued down the hall.

At Lisa's room, Gavin observed immediately that Lisa had fallen asleep. Jessie was leaning close to her, humming a song. When she saw him, she stopped.

"You don't have to quit on my account," he said, his voice rougher than he intended.

Jessie stood. "She's asleep. She needs that more than anything else right now. Uh, I'd like to talk to you. Can we step outside for a minute?"

"Jessie, we're both tired. Maybe it should wait."

"Please, Gavin, I don't want to wait." Her blue eyes were pleading.

He hesitated a moment, then motioned her into the hall.

Jessie closed the heavy door partway but stood in the opening so she could hear if Lisa made a sound. "First of all, I want to tell you how grateful I am for everything you did."

He closed his eyes for a moment. "I don't want your gratitude, Jessie."

She took a deep breath and clenched her hands in front of her. "No, I know you don't. I want to give you more than gratitude. I want to give you my trust and my love."

His heart ached. He wanted to believe her, but wanting for either of them might not be enough. "Jessie..."

"Please listen to me, Gavin. You were right about my father and me. He tried to control me. I fought against it but didn't stop it. Now I have. I told him if he interferes in my life or Lisa's again, I'll cut him off from both of us."

A flicker of hope ignited in Gavin's heart. "What did he say?"

"We were in the middle of it when the accident happened. But afterward I told him again I love you and if he can't accept that, then he can't be part of my life."

There was a strength in Jessie's words, on her face, that Gavin had never seen before.

She rushed on. "Gavin, I don't know if you can forgive me for my doubts, my lack of trust, but I'm hoping you can. Because I do love you and I do trust you. When I saw Lisa lying in the street, I only thought of you, having you take care of her, having you by my side.''

Gavin knew Lisa was more precious to Jessie than her own life. In a flash, he heard Owen Windsor's words. *Jessie called for you. Remember that.* An olive branch possibly? An admission that Jessie had made her choice, and he accepted it?

All the love Gavin had ever felt for Jessie overflowed his heart. ''You know I'd move heaven and earth for you and Lisa.''

Jessie nodded. ''I know. Do you know how much I love you? That I *do* trust you? That Lisa and I will move to Denver with you if that's what you want?''

Gavin gazed into Jessie's eyes and saw she meant every word. He saw everything he'd ever hoped to see. With his chest tightening so painfully he could hardly breathe, he wrapped her in his arms and kissed her with all the love, all the joy, all the passion and all the trust he'd seen mirrored in her eyes.

Jessie kissed him the same way, holding nothing back, giving and taking and sharing.

Finally Gavin raised his head and held her face between his palms. ''I love you.''

She wrapped her arms around his neck and stood on tiptoe to kiss him again. He let her initiate, let her wield the power she'd found in their love, until his own desire drove him to press her tighter against him, to return the strokes of her tongue harder and longer, to break off the kiss before he couldn't.

Resting his forehead against hers, he said, ''I want to get married *as soon as possible.*''

She smiled. "As soon as we can get a license, or as soon as we can get a church and reception hall?"

He groaned. "I suppose the church and reception are important to you?"

She stroked his jaw. "I only intend to get married once. I'd like it to be in a church before God and our friends."

He covered her hand with his. "You're a wise lady."

She shook her head. "Just a lady in love."

"Maybe I'll spend the night holding you in that bed next to Lisa's. It sure would give the grapevine something to talk about tomorrow."

Jessie laughed. "If I thought we could stop at holding, I'd agree, despite the grapevine."

He curved his arm around her waist. "Let's go watch our daughter sleep. And talk about the future."

Jessie leaned her head against his shoulder as they walked into their daughter's room. Gavin knew there would be plenty of time for holding and kissing and making love. A lifetime.

Epilogue

As the organ music swelled, Jessie took her father's arm. In her gown of ivory silk with its fitted bodice and beaded-lace sleeves, she felt like a princess. Her father leaned toward her. "You're a beautiful bride."

She smiled up at him, thankful he seemed more content these days, grateful Gavin had accepted his overtures for peace between them.

Jessie and her father started down the white runner.

Gavin and Jessie had discussed moving to Denver. But after weighing the pros and cons, they'd decided to stay in Four Oaks. Gavin wanted Lisa to have roots. In Four Oaks, she did—her friends, her neighbors, her grandfather. Jessie's practice was well established. Gavin liked living near Nathan and within a few hours of Jeff and Katie. So they'd made the decision to stay in Four Oaks whether or not Peter Winnichuk retired. Just last week, Gavin had gotten the call in which Peter formally decided to spend his golden years with his wife, traveling and playing golf.

The pews in the back of the church stood empty. Jessie and Gavin had decided to keep the guest list small. But as she and her father approached the middle of the church, she realized everyone who mattered to them had come.

Gavin had asked a few colleagues and their wives and husbands, as had Jessie. She smiled at them. As she neared the front pews, she saw Cade and Randi and their boys, Jeff and Katie with their infant and Ted with Marly. Shannon, her matron of honor, and Lisa—the cutest flower girl she'd ever seen—stood to the left. Nathan, Gavin's best man, smiled at her.

And then her gaze met Gavin's.

It had been seven weeks since that night in the hospital, seven weeks to talk and plan and hold and kiss...but not make love. They'd decided to wait until tonight...until they drove to Jeff and Katie's cabin. Joy overwhelmed Jessie, and tears filled her eyes.

Her father stopped when they reached Gavin. He shook Gavin's hand and then he placed hers in the clasp of her husband-to-be. His voice husky, he said to both of them, "Be happy."

From the look in Gavin's eyes, the firm grip of his fingers, Jessie knew they would be, no matter what life dealt them. They'd loved each other too long and risked too much not to hold on, appreciate and revel in what they shared.

Jessie handed Shannon her bouquet and then turned to face the minister.

For Jessie, the ceremony passed much too quickly. Gavin's husky vows, hers to him, the exchange of rings, seemed to be over before she hardly took a breath. Yet she knew she'd remember the day forever.

When the minister pronounced them husband and wife and said to Gavin, "You may now kiss your bride," their guests clapped. The applause, the church and the minister faded away as Gavin slipped his fingers under her veil, lifted it over her head and gave her a long, lingering kiss that took Jessie on the beginning of a journey, a journey they'd complete tonight.

Nathan cleared his throat. "Hey, you two. We'd like to get to the reception sometime today."

Gavin raised his head and smiled. "My best man is performing his duties too well." As he turned with Jessie to face their guests and renewed applause broke out, he reached for Lisa's hand.

Lisa's face beamed as she realized she could walk down the aisle with them. She stepped in front of Gavin, smiled at Jessie, then said importantly to Nathan, "He's my dad."

Nathan chuckled. "I know. You couldn't have a better one."

Jessie and Gavin walked down the aisle, holding their daughter's hands. As Jessie carried Lisa's basket of rose petals and her own bouquet, Gavin gazed at her with so much love her breath caught.

He was her first love, her only love.

For always.

*   *   *   *   *

THE BEST MEN *series continues as Nathan jumps onto the marriage wagon. Watch for* A GROOM AND A PROMISE, *available in October from Silhouette Romance.*

This October, be the first to read these wonderful authors as they make their dazzling debuts!

Women to Watch

THE WEDDING KISS by Robin Wells
(Silhouette Romance #1185)
A reluctant bachelor rescues the woman he loves from the man she's about to marry—and turns into a willing groom himself!

THE SEX TEST by Patty Salier
(Silhouette Desire #1032)
A pretty professor learns there's more to making love than meets the eye when she takes lessons from a sexy stranger.

IN A FAMILY WAY by Julia Mozingo
(Special Edition #1062)
A woman without a past finds shelter in the arms of a handsome rancher. Can she trust him to protect her unborn child?

UNDER COVER OF THE NIGHT by Roberta Tobeck
(Intimate Moments #744)
A rugged government agent encounters the woman he has always loved. But past secrets could threaten their future.

DATELESS IN DALLAS by Samantha Carter
(Yours Truly)
A hapless reporter investigates how to find the perfect mate—and winds up falling for her handsome rival!

Don't miss the brightest stars of tomorrow!

Only from **V** *Silhouette®*
TM

MILLION DOLLAR SWEEPSTAKES
AND EXTRA BONUS PRIZE DRAWING

Who can resist a Texan...or a Calloway?

This September, award-winning author
ANNETTE BROADRICK
returns to Texas, with a brand-new
story about the Calloways...

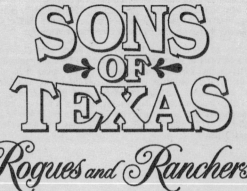

SONS OF TEXAS

Rogues and Ranchers

CLINT: The brave leader. Used to keeping secrets.

CADE: The Lone Star Stud. Used to having women
fall at his feet...

MATT: The family guardian. Used to handling
trouble...

They must discover the identity of the mystery
woman with Calloway eyes—and uncover a
conspiracy that threatens their family....

Look for **SONS OF TEXAS:** Rogues and Ranchers
in September 1996!

Only from Silhouette...where passion lives.

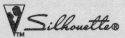

SOMETIMES BIG SURPRISES
COME IN SMALL PACKAGES!

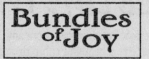

Bundles of Joy

THE MAN WHO WOULD BE DADDY

by

Marie Ferrarella

He'd rescued her baby! Single mom Christa Winslow couldn't
thank Malcolm Evans enough. But could this handsome hero
help mother and child once again? Christa knew her little girl
needed a father and that beneath Malcolm's gruff exterior
lay the tender soul of a man who would be daddy....

Don't miss this adorable **Bundles of Joy,**
available in September, only from

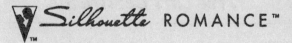

Silhouette ROMANCE™

As seen on TV!
Free Gift Offer

With a Free Gift proof-of-purchase from any Silhouette® book,
you can receive a beautiful cubic zirconia pendant.

This gorgeous marquise-shaped stone is a genuine cubic
zirconia—accented by an 18" gold tone necklace.

(Approximate retail value $19.95)

Send for yours today...
compliments of ▼ *Silhouette*®

To receive your free gift, a cubic zirconia pendant, send us one original proof-of-
purchase, photocopies not accepted, from the back of any Silhouette Romance™,
Silhouette Desire®, Silhouette Special Edition®, Silhouette Intimate Moments®
or Silhouette Yours Truly™ title available in August, September or October at your favorite
retail outlet, together with the Free Gift Certificate, plus a check or money order for
$1.65 U.S./$2.15 CAN. (do not send cash) to cover postage and handling, payable
to Silhouette Free Gift Offer. We will send you the specified gift. Allow 6 to 8 weeks for
delivery. Offer good until October 31, 1996 or while quantities last. Offer valid in the
U.S. and Canada only.

Free Gift Certificate

Name: _____

Address: _____

City: _____ State/Province: _____ Zip/Postal Code: _____

Mail this certificate, one proof-of-purchase and a check or money order for postage
and handling to: SILHOUETTE FREE GIFT OFFER 1996. In the U.S.: 3010 Walden
Avenue, P.O. Box 9077, Buffalo NY 14269-9077. In Canada: P.O. Box 613, Fort Erie,
Ontario L2Z 5X3.

FREE GIFT OFFER   084-KMD

ONE PROOF-OF-PURCHASE

To collect your fabulous FREE GIFT, a cubic zirconia pendant, you must include this
original proof-of-purchase for each gift with the property completed Free Gift Certificate.

084-KMD

FORTUNE'S Children™

Bestselling Author

MERLINE LOVELACE

Continues the twelve-book series—FORTUNE'S CHILDREN
in September 1996 with Book Three

BEAUTY AND THE BODYGUARD

Ex-mercenary Rafe Stone was Fortune Cosmetics cover girl
Allie Fortune's best protection against an obsessed stalker. He
was also the one man this tempting beauty was willing to risk
her heart for....

MEET THE FORTUNES—a family whose legacy is greater than
riches. Because where there's a will...there's a *wedding!*

*A CASTING CALL TO
ALL FORTUNE'S CHILDREN FANS!*
If you are truly one of the fortunate
few, you may win a trip to
Los Angeles to audition for
Wheel of Fortune®. Look for
details in all retail Fortune's Children titles!

Look us up on-line at: http://www.romance.net

You're About to Become a

Privileged Woman

Reap the rewards of fabulous free gifts and
benefits with proofs-of-purchase from
Silhouette and Harlequin books

Pages & Privileges™

It's our way of thanking you for
buying our books at your
favorite retail stores.

PROOF OF PURCHASE
SR-PP171
Offer expires October 31, 1996

Pages & Privileges ™

Harlequin and Silhouette—
the most privileged readers in the world!

For more information about Harlequin and
Silhouette's PAGES & PRIVILEGES program call the
Pages & Privileges Benefits Desk: 1-503-794-2499

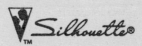

Silhouette®

SR-PP171